COWBOY'S CHRISTMAS NANNY

TRINITY FALLS SWEET ROMANCE - BOOK 1

CLARA PINES

PINE NUT PRESS

Copyright © 2022 by Pine Nut Press

All rights reserved. This book or any portion thereof may not be reproduced or used in any manner whatsoever without the express written permission of the publisher except for the use of brief quotations in a book review.

13th Story Press

PO Box 506

Swarthmore, PA 19081

13thStoryPress@gmail.com

Cover designed by The Book Brander

1

NATALIE

Natalie Bell walked along Park Avenue as lazy snowflakes drifted down, kissing the sandstone sidewalks of her hometown, and melting as they landed.

It was a little early in the season for snow to stick. But the big candy cane decorations already hung from the lampposts, and the Victorian dollhouse in the town real estate office window was decked out with Christmas lights, a sure sign that the holidays were fast approaching.

Things in Trinity Falls never seemed to change.

That same dollhouse had been in that window ever since Natalie was a little girl. She remembered pressing her nose against the glass to admire it while her Nana chuckled.

Well, most things didn't change.

She swallowed over the lump in her throat and smoothed down her ponytail for the tenth time since she'd left the house five minutes ago.

Natalie normally wore her hair down, and just a touch of make-up. But today she was interviewing for a job at the café in town, and she wanted to make sure she looked very serious and ready to work.

Most people here probably remembered her as more of a dreamer than a worker. But the last couple of years had pretty much wrung that out of her.

After graduation, she had left Pennsylvania for New York City with not much more than an acoustic guitar and a determination to share her music with the world.

But a few years later, she had nothing to show for it but a revolving cast of snobby roommates, a job at a greasy diner in the city, and an endless run of open mic nights under her belt.

It wasn't much of a life, but she'd been getting by just fine, until Dr. Wilkinson had called to let her know that her Nana wasn't well.

Carla Bell wouldn't have told her granddaughter she needed help for anything. But the town doctor guessed correctly that Natalie would want to know.

So, she had given up her pathetic city life without a second thought in order to be with Nana. And she would have done so just as quickly, even if she had made it big.

Her parents had passed when she was so little that she barely remembered them. But Nana had stepped right in and given Natalie and her big brother a happy life of simple pleasures in Trinity Falls.

Natalie and Chris had never wanted for a single thing. And although it was just the three of them, Nana made it feel like they had the biggest, warmest family in the world.

The little house on Park Avenue was always full of life, and the smell of something delicious in the oven. Nana hosted a book club, coordinated a driving service for the visually impaired, and, along with her tight crew of older ladies, basically had a hand in every good thing that happened in Trinity Falls.

Holidays were especially full of happy, busy tasks, and there was always a houseful of Nana's strays who had no place else to go - like the family from Central America spending a year in Trinity Falls, or the Malones during the winter they lost their house. And there was the one incredible year when someone had a kitchen fire on Christmas Eve in the apartment building across the alleyway from Nana's bungalow.

The firefighters escorted all the families out to the icy parking lot. And Nana had Natalie and Chris walk them right through the back gate and across the yard to her house for cookies and hot chocolate. The house was filled to the brim that night, and all the kids slept out on the sunporch, with so many of them out there giggling that the usually frigid space was warm.

Natalie had come home this spring, thinking she'd have a few years to show Nana the same compassion and good cheer she had shared with others her whole life.

Instead, Nana had deteriorated swiftly. She was gone before it was time to visit the orchard and buy apple cider to put in the crock for the town Halloween Hop.

Chris, who had joined the military, hadn't even made it home to say goodbye. It had just been the two of them.

"I love you, Natalie," Nana had whispered at the end. "Promise me two things."

"Of course," Natalie whispered back, holding her tears in. "Anything."

"Promise me you'll make sure your brother knows I love him," Nana said. "And promise that you won't stay in my house moping around. You're full of life, my girl. You've got to get out there and live it."

I'm trying, Nana, she promised inwardly.

But that promise had turned out to be a lot harder to keep than she'd expected.

Natalie had spent the last couple of months since the funeral telling herself that she would just get the house ready to sell, and then move on.

But it was too hard to give away Nana's clothing, to get rid of her sweet collection of china pigs, and her excess of baking tools. A massive assortment of sweet romance novels they had collected from the library book sales over the years overflowed the shelves and were stacked on the floor of the tiny alcove Nana loved to call *the library*. Natalie found it impossible to even think about donating them. She and Nana had read some of those books so many times that Natalie thought of the characters as her friends.

She found herself starting with the basement and the garage, working her way through things that probably didn't matter, to avoid the ones that would tug at her heart.

But the outside world kept moving, and the county tax on the house was due in January. Maybe it was a blessing that she had to find work in order to pay. It forced her into motion.

Already, she felt strangely peaceful, walking in the snow past so many familiar sights from her childhood. Nana's house was in the last block of residential homes before the village began. So, they had always been right next to what passed for hustle and bustle in a town the size of Trinity Falls.

Each house and each storefront had its own story. She remembered following Chris and his friends, tagging along when they brought coins to the Co-op grocery story for ice cream bars, and later, when they were old enough, walking all the way to the pool and the pizza shop afterward.

By then, she had gone from hero-worshipping Chris and his friends to crushing on one of them.

I wonder where Shane Cassidy is now...

Shane was super smart, athletic, and just plain nice, even if he was a little quiet. They had both been counselors at the local camp for two summers, and she had loved seeing how gentle he was with the littlest kids, helping them feel at home away from home.

Most likely, he had moved on from Trinity Falls and was living a fancier life in the city someplace. With his grades and talents, he had surely outgrown Trinity Falls.

His family, the Cassidys, owned the local farm where she and Nana and the rest of the town went for cider and bushels of apples every fall. Every girl she knew had been crushing on one or another of the Cassidy boys at some point.

But Natalie had only ever had eyes for Shane.

He had always been nice to her, but he also only treated her like Chris's little sister. She was invisible to him as a woman.

It's probably for the best.

Invisibility was probably her strongest quality at the moment. But she was determined to turn that around.

A job at the local café might not be anything to brag about, but her best friend from high school worked there, and it would get her out of Nana's house and into the world, just like she promised.

After that, it was only a matter of figuring out what she actually wanted to do with her life, and putting a plan into action.

By this time next year, I'll make you proud, Nana.

Reminding herself that she had this under control, Natalie pushed open the door to Jolly Beans, and sucked in a breath of delicious, coffee-scented air.

2

NATALIE

The bells jingled merrily over her head as Natalie entered, announcing her arrival in the little coffee shop. A few of the patrons looked over to see who it was, and a handful of those she knew gave her a friendly nod, then turned back to their conversations.

Christmas music drifted down from the ancient speakers in the corners. But there was a year-round, festive atmosphere to the place that Natalie had always liked.

The location of the café right next to the train station meant they saw a brisk business in to-go orders during rush hour, and plenty of sit-down business from stay-at-home moms, retirees, and community college kids all day long.

"Hey Holly," she called out when she spotted her best friend from high school.

The pretty blonde grinned up at her from behind the counter where she was pouring out the last of a pot of coffee. Natalie knew she probably should have spent more time with Holly since coming back to town. But she hadn't really been in the mood to do much socializing.

"How's it going?" Holly asked. "Are you here for the reason I think you're here?"

"I was just looking for Pete," Natalie said with a wink.

"*Yes*," Holly said, her blue eyes twinkling. She had been trying to convince Natalie to come in for an interview for months now. "He's in back, helping the kitchen with the order for this ten-top."

She nodded down at the massive tray of drinks on the counter and then indicated a huge table of professors from the community college.

"Want to come back here and start me a new pot of coffee?" Holly asked. "Might as well get used to the equipment."

"Sure," Natalie said, happy to help.

In all reality, she probably could have aimed a little higher than the local coffee shop for a job, since she had waited tables for real in New York. She could have at least interviewed at a pub in one of the bigger towns, where she could make better tips.

But working here with Holly was just what she needed to get herself out of the rut she'd been in. And there was something comforting about being in Trinity Falls over the holidays.

She slipped behind the counter and grabbed a filter and a scoop for the coffee.

"Cricket?" a familiar deep voice said. "Cricket Bell?"

It can't be.

But no one else called her Cricket.

She glanced up... and up, and up into the beautiful blue eyes of a very handsome, very grown-up Shane Cassidy.

He had to be six feet tall, with the same indigo eyes and dark hair that fell just a little too long over his eyes. His shoulders were wide, and she could see the brawn of his upper arms bulging through the red and brown flannel he wore.

"Daddy," squeaked another voice. "I thought we were going to the nut store."

She glanced down to see a tiny girl, probably just three or four years old, tugging at his hand.

Each pull tugged at Natalie's heartstrings just a little.

In some alternate universe, she could have been my daughter.

She ripped her eyes back up to Shane's, feeling foolish and unsure where a thought like that would even come from.

She wasn't a schoolgirl anymore. She should be way past the time of daydreaming impossible futures with her crush. The alternate universe she was picturing was one where she would have had to have the confidence to march right up to him and tell him how she felt back in school. And that was something she never would have done.

Plus, he would have had to feel the same way.

"It's great to see you," he said. "I didn't know you were staying in town."

"I've been kind of wrapped up with the house," she admitted.

"I'm so sorry about your Nana," he told her. "We were at her service, but we didn't want to fight the crowd to say hi."

"Thank you," she said, swallowing hard. Somehow sympathy always made her grief worse. "And who is this?"

"I'm Rumor," the little girl said happily. "My daddy has to buy something so I can use the bathroom."

"I'll take a cup of coffee," he said with a wry grin. "If that's okay."

"Oh, I don't work here," she said.

He gave her an odd look.

It suddenly hit her that she was standing behind the counter in a plain white blouse, making coffee.

"Shane Cassidy," someone said happily, with a sharp, rural Pennsylvania twang.

Shane was distracted momentarily, so she took the opportunity to gather herself and finish fixing the coffee.

"Hey, Reggie," Shane said.

"If you're here to check the board, don't even bother," Reggie Webb told him. "That new guy's hiring anything with a pulse. You won't find help this season."

"Daddy," Rumor said quietly.

"I know, Reggie," Shane said. "Can't blame a guy for trying though, right? I need to get my daughter—"

"Now I personally can't figure out why he chose now to start up a new place like that," Reggie went on in a just-starting-to-chew-the-fat way, oblivious to the fact that Shane was trying to get away.

"Daddy," Rumor said, her little voice more urgent now.

"Would you look at that, she has her mother's eyes," Reggie said. "That takes me back to a story I might have told you before, about her great grand-pappy."

Natalie quickly pressed the button for the coffee to brew and slipped out from behind the counter.

Rumor was squirming a little now, and Shane looked torn between respecting the older farmer and taking off with his daughter before she had an accident.

"Do you want me to take you to the bathroom, sweetie?" Natalie asked, bending down.

Rumor nodded enthusiastically.

Natalie glanced up at Shane in question, and he gave her a grateful look that made her cheeks burn.

"Come on," she told the little one.

They headed off to the nook at the back of the café, and

Natalie pointed her to the women's powder room.

"How do you know that's the right one?" Rumor asked.

"Look at the drawings on the door," Natalie said. "The one with the dress is for ladies."

"It looks like a cape," Rumor said wisely. "For superheroes!"

"Do you need me to come in with you?" Natalie asked, trying to hide her smile.

"No, you stay right there and watch the door," Rumor said. "That's what my daddy does."

"Okay, I'll be right here," Natalie agreed. "You yell if you need me. My name is Natalie."

Rumor scowled at her and then darted into the bathroom before she could ask what was wrong.

Natalie knew from experience that it was a plain one-seater bathroom, and there wasn't much trouble to get into, but she kept a sharp ear on the door anyway while she scanned the café.

The professors at the ten-top were all laughing and enjoying their coffees and teas. She wondered if they were there on business, or just to enjoy each other's company.

At a nearby booth, a tired looking mom with a kid about Rumor's age and a baby in a stroller was doing her best to keep them both content while she pounded what looked like a latte and texted frantically on a phone with a hot pink case.

Holly was moving with quiet confidence around the space, dropping off extra napkins and glasses of water, and clearing up empty paper cups.

Natalie tried to pay attention to what Holly was doing, but her eyes kept moving to where Shane stood by Reggie. The older man was now leaning against the counter, presumably to reserve all his energy for talking.

Shane exuded patience and interest. She understood why Reggie Webb delighted in talking to him.

It was interesting that Shane was here looking for help. It must mean he had stayed local and was involved in running the family farm. She had been so certain the pride of the Cassidy clan would be in the city chasing dollar signs in a fancy office building.

There's no place like home, Nana liked to say, and she was always talking about Trinity Falls when she did.

Natalie had taken the town for granted growing up here. But being back and seeing the way people greeted each other and stopped to talk made her realize how cold and gray New York had been. The whole city seemed to be made up of gray sidewalks, gray buildings, and people who were all elbows and e-cigarettes.

The sound of the toilet flushing snapped her out of her thoughts and back to the present. A few seconds later, she was pleased to hear water running for long enough that it was clear Rumor had washed her hands.

"All done," the little girl announced as she marched victoriously out.

Natalie glanced over at Shane, but it looked like Reggie was still knee-deep in his story. The Webbs were talkers.

"Hey, I think there's a snowflake making station by the big window," Natalie said. "I was going to check it out. Want to make one with me?"

"Really?" Rumor said, her eyes getting big. "Sure!"

"Let your daddy know where we're headed, okay?" Natalie said.

Rumor dashed through the crowded café to her dad.

"We're gonna make snowflakes," she told him.

He nodded to her and then glanced up to Natalie and mouthed *thank you*.

She wanted to melt at the sweet look on his masculine face.

Stop that. He's a family man.

Biting her lip, she focused her attention on her new friend, who was already grabbing sheets of paper and rummaging around for the scissors.

"Do you want to know the key to making an amazing snowflake?" Natalie asked.

"Yes," Rumor said, turning to her so fast her chestnut curls bounced on her shoulders.

"You have to start with a square piece of paper, not a rectangle," Natalie told her.

"A square," Rumor echoed.

She grabbed the scissors and did a pretty good job cutting the top off a piece of paper. But when she held it up, she frowned.

"That's not a square," she said indignantly.

"It's *almost* a perfect square," Natalie told her encouragingly. "Do you want me to try to make it a little better? Or do you want to do it yourself?"

"Self," Rumor proclaimed, applying herself to the task without waiting for acknowledgement.

The end result was a little better, though still crooked.

"It's still not right," Rumor said sadly.

"I think it's great," Natalie told her. "No two snowflakes are alike. So, this will make it more like a real snowflake, right?"

Rumor nodded, though she didn't look convinced.

"Now we're going to fold it up," Natalie said. "I'll do one too, so you can see."

She cut herself a square, careful not to make it too perfect, and made the first fold.

Rumor imitated her without being asked.

"Great," Natalie said. "Now another."

Slowly and carefully, she did the four folding steps she and Nana had learned watching a holiday home decor special back when she was in high school.

Rumor followed right along, concentrating so hard that a cute little furrow formed in her brow.

"Now we cut the points off, like this," Natalie said.

Rumor watched and then did hers, too.

"And now we have the basic shape," Natalie said. "We can just trim away wherever it feels right. Do you have any questions?"

"If you're called Cricket, why did you tell me your name is Natalie?" Rumor asked, her blue eyes flashing up to Natalie's.

"Oh," Natalie said, surprised. "My real name is Natalie. But your dad used to call me Cricket when we were kids."

"Why?" Rumor asked, seemingly unsurprised that all the grown-ups in town knew her daddy.

"My brother used to call me *Nat* for short," she explained. "But it sounds like gnat, the bug. And I used to yell that I didn't want to be a gnat."

"Yeah," Rumor said, as if she agreed. "Did he stop?"

"Nope, Chris didn't care," Natalie laughed. "But your daddy asked me if I didn't want to be a gnat, what *did* I want to be. And I was reading a book at school about a cricket, so I said I wanted to be a cricket. And from then on, he started calling me Cricket."

"That's silly," Rumor said with a big smile.

"I know," Natalie said. "But it made me really happy."

"Hey ladies, what are you up to?" Shane asked in his deep, friendly voice.

Natalie wondered how long he'd been standing there.

3

NATALIE

Natalie looked up to see Shane standing over them, a smile tugging at the corners of his mouth.

"Making snowflakes," Rumor said, applying herself to her snowflake as industriously as if she were being paid by the snip.

"Thank you so much," Shane said to Natalie.

"It's my pleasure," she told him honestly. "I'm just waiting for Pete to be done so I can interview. But I think it's going to be a while, since they're getting a massive order ready for that big table."

"You're looking for work?" Shane asked.

She nodded.

"Well, word to the wise, hold out for decent pay," Shane said. "A guy from the city just bought Livingston Farm. He's hired so many people that it's hard to find decent workers right now. So, you've got some leverage."

"You're hiring?" she asked. She hadn't been able to help overhearing, but it seemed more polite not to say so directly.

"Hands for the farm," he nodded. "Or at least I'm trying

to. That's what Reggie wanted to chat about. I'm really squeezed this season."

"You're working with your parents now?" she asked, charmed at the idea that he spent his days at the farm she and Nana had visited so often.

"I'm running the whole thing myself now," he said with a half-smile. "My parents wanted to retire and live it up. We have a crew for the store, and one for the entertainment, but they all report to me."

At a small table next to the ten-top an awkward looking boy stood up and held up a stack of poster boards, clearly preparing to launch into a full-blown prom-posal. Although technically, the upcoming dance wasn't a prom. Natalie supposed that made it a Snow-Ball-posal, but that was probably not as good as a hashtag. His buddies all had their cell phones out, filming him as he began reading each of the posters out loud, while the girl on the receiving end giggled and squealed.

"So sweet," Natalie said, smiling and shaking her head.

She was secretly kind of glad no one did that kind of thing when she was still in school. It seemed like an awful lot of pressure. But then an image of Shane putting on a big show for her popped into her mind, and her cheeks got hot.

"Yeah," Shane said, snapping her out of her thoughts. "Kids are something else."

She realized she'd been staring at him, and tore her eyes away, feeling even more embarrassed.

"Well, I wish I had the know-how to help you, but waiting tables is more my speed than caring for horses," she told him. "I appreciate the advice though."

There was a moment of silence between them.

Just as it was about to cross into awkward territory, Pete came out of the back, carrying a giant tray of lunches.

"That's my cue," she said. "It was really fun to hang out with you, Rumor."

"Aren't we going to open our snowflakes?" Rumor asked.

"Of course," Natalie said. "You can do the honors."

Rumor carefully peeled open her snowflake and a waterfall of happy laughter flowed from her as the cut-up square of paper unfolded into a lacy wonder.

"That tickled you, huh, Rumor?" Shane asked, chuckling. "It's really pretty."

"Very nice," Natalie told her. "I have to run, but I'm sure I'll be seeing you around town. Can you open mine for me?"

"Sure," Rumor chirped. "Bye, Cricket."

She gave the little girl a wink and a wave and then scooted through the tables.

Pete was setting down the three plates from his tray in front of the customers by the head of the table. She moved to the counter, so when he was done he would see her, and tried her best not to look back at Shane, no matter how much she wanted to.

"Here," Pete said, waving her over.

She started to jog to him and slammed into something. Hard.

Everything seemed to slide into slow motion after that.

Pain bloomed in her left shoulder. Someone squealed. Silverware hit the floor like bells chiming, followed by the crash of china, and hollow sound of two trays spinning on the hardwood floor.

She blinked back into reality to see Holly practically spread-eagle on the floor in front of her. She must have had at least three lunches on each of her two trays. The amount of food and porcelain shards on the floor was incredible.

The teens at the back table began giggling.

Pete hadn't been calling Natalie over. He'd been waving to Holly.

"H-Holly," Natalie stammered. "I'm s-o sorry. Let me help you."

Holly pulled herself up to a sitting position. "I'm fine," she said.

Thankfully, she looked okay, other than the food in her hair. Though she did seem a little dazed.

Natalie was already picking up handfuls of the mess and placing them on one of the trays, her body moving automatically.

"I'll pay for these meals," she told her friend as hot tears threatened to burst from her eyes. "I'm so sorry."

"No," Pete yelled, marching up to her. "No, no, no. Put that stuff down and get up."

"I'll clean it up," she tried to tell him. "It's my fault."

"Absolutely not," he said sharply. "You don't work here. You're a liability. Just get out of the way."

His tone was so angry and frustrated that she didn't dare speak another word.

She just scrambled to her feet, brushed herself off and ran for the door of the café, wishing she could disappear into the center of the earth instead of just out onto Park Avenue.

The door opened, letting in a blast of cold air and a puff of lazy snowflakes. The overhead bell jingled happily again, as if to taunt her.

She made it just a few steps down the sidewalk before a big hand closed around her shoulder.

"Natalie," a deep voice said.

She turned to see Shane, with Rumor in tow.

"Are you okay?" he demanded.

"I'm fine," she said, sighing. "Just embarrassed. And jobless."

"About that," he said, fixing her in his blue gaze and seeming to consider for a moment. "Would you be interested in working as a nanny, on a temporary basis?"

She blinked at him for a few seconds, her brain refusing to compute.

"Just for the holiday season," he said. "Until I can find some help on the farm. I wanted to hire hands so I could spend more time with the kids, but since I know how to work with the horses, and you're great with kids, this seems meant to be."

"I don't have experience working with kids," she said.

"Like fun you don't," he chuckled. "You were the most popular junior counselor at Trinity Falls Day Camp."

The memory made her smile. She had loved being a camp counselor, playing songs for the kids to sing to on the acoustic guitar Nana had bought her at the church thrift shop.

And Shane had been a counselor too, a few years ahead of her. She remembered the flashes of hot jealousy she felt when her little charges *shipped* him with another senior counselor.

"That was a long time ago," she told him.

"Our snowflakes are next to each other," Rumor told her suddenly, pointing at the store front.

Sure enough, two paper snowflakes at just about Rumor height had been taped to the window together. And suddenly, Natalie felt a small spark of hope, and maybe something else that she wasn't ready to admit.

"I would be taking care of Rumor?" she asked, gazing fondly at the curly little head.

"And my son, Wyatt," Shane said. "But he's thirteen, so you won't see much of him."

That was a sad idea, and one that might need exploring.

"When would you need me to start?" she asked.

"Come by tomorrow morning," Shane said. "As early as you can would be great."

"Don't you need to talk to your wife?" she asked. "She'll want to interview me."

Now it was his turn to blink at her for a moment.

"My mommy died in an *accident*," Rumor whispered loudly.

Shame flooded her veins. This was the terrible cherry on top of the most mortifying ten minutes of her life.

"I'm so sorry, Rumor," Natalie told the child, wishing she could go back in time and cut out her own tongue. "I didn't know."

"You've been away a long time," Shane said with the compassion she should have been giving him, given the situation. "Anyway, come on by first thing. We'll be glad to see you. You know where the farm is, right?"

"Yes," she said stupidly. She and Nana had been so many times.

"We're in the new house, behind the big red barn," he told her.

"I'll be there," she promised.

He rewarded her with the smile she remembered, brilliant, warm, and so wide it crinkled his eyes at the corners.

"Bye, Cricket," Rumor yelled to her for the second time before they headed to a late model pick-up truck. "See you tomorrow!"

4

SHANE

Shane loaded Rumor into the truck, his hands automatically tugging on the buckles of her carseat to be sure she was nice and snug.

But his mind was racing with thoughts of Natalie.

"Where are we going, Daddy?" Rumor asked, tearing him out of his fantasies and back to reality.

"We're going to go visit Grandma and Grandpa," he told her. "We might have to skip the nut store today. Grandma wants to make plans for the holidays with you."

"Cookies," Rumor yelled, all other plans forgotten.

He closed her door and got into the driver's seat, hoping he had distracted her with enough grandma thoughts that he could keep her off the subject of Cricket Bell.

One of his daughter's greatest gifts was an uncanny ability to read his emotions. And while he had nothing to hide, per se, he still wanted to unpack his feelings about Cricket on his own rather than out loud with his precocious four-year-old.

He turned on the radio and smiled when Rumor started singing along with the Christmas carols right away.

He'd lost Lou around the holidays, and this time of year sometimes made him feel a little off-balance, usually when he least expected it. A particular song would come on, or he'd catch the scent of cookies baking, and it would feel like he had just gotten the call that she was never coming home again.

Rumor loved everything about Christmas, though. And he wouldn't dampen her enjoyment for the world. With the light flurries falling around them, it was downright jolly.

As her little voice chirped about the joys of sleigh riding, he let himself think for just a minute about Cricket Bell.

Her older brother, Chris, had been his best friend since the first day of kindergarten, when he spotted Chris's triceratops eraser and lifted his own T-rex eraser from his pencil box to greet it.

At first, Cricket had been Chris's cute baby sister, with her dark brown hair and big eyes. He remembered her clambering up to take a spot on the sofa between them while they watched cartoons, her chubby hand wrapping absently around Chris's or patting his back.

By the time they were in middle school, she was in first grade and tagged along as much as Chris would let her. She would get frustrated when they rode their bikes where she wasn't allowed to follow. But she and their Nana would usually end up baking something special, which she was proud to offer to her brother and his friend when they inevitably came back muddy and ravenous from their adventures in the woods.

At some point during high school, he started noticing that Cricket wasn't a baby anymore. As a matter of fact, she was growing up to be quite pretty, with her dark hair and hazel eyes. She was quieter than before, but doted on her brother as much as ever, and she was always happy to see Shane and give him a shy smile.

He watched her with the kids at Trinity Falls Day Camp when she got a coveted position as a junior counselor. She was kind and gentle, quick to laugh, and slow to lose her patience.

But the night of the Snow Ball dance, when she was in eighth grade and he was a senior, sealed his fate.

He and Chris were taking the Webb twins, Jenna and MaryLou. They had gathered at Chris's place, since his Nana always welcomed the teens.

He happened to be in the foyer, taking his phone off the charger, when Cricket came down the stairs in her dress.

Shane wasn't the most fashion-conscious kid, but he would never forget that gown, a sea foam green that highlighted her creamy skin and bright eyes. It was a modest length, and covered her far more than the faded swimsuit he'd seen her in plenty of times down at the lake.

But something about the way it cinched at her waist and flared at her hips into rivulets of soft-looking tulle took his breath away. She looked like a beautiful angel.

For a moment he wasn't a teenager. He was a man, gazing up at the woman who was going to take his heart.

Then she spotted him and turned red from her forehead down to her clavicle.

"Shane," she said, with an awkward smile.

"I didn't know you were coming," he said stupidly.

"Brad Williams invited me," she told him, gathering the gown in one hand like a princess and descending the rest of the stairs.

Shane suddenly wanted to punch Brad Williams in the nose, and he wasn't even sure why. Brad was a little preppy, but had always been a decent guy.

"Holy wow, Nat," Chris had yelled as he walked in and saw his sister in her dress. "You look like a giant cake."

"Stop calling me Nat," she moaned, rolling her eyes.

"You look great, Williams is going to lose his mind," Chris laughed. "But make sure he knows I'll punch him in the nose if he gets fresh with my baby sister."

That made sense. Chris had the right to punch people in the nose on Cricket's behalf. Shane didn't.

As a matter of fact, the way his mind had been working would have made Chris was to punch *him* in the nose if he'd known.

"Hi guys," Jenna Webb yelled as she and MaryLou came in, wearing their hot pink and black dresses.

In the commotion, Cricket had escaped his attention, but he would never forget that night and the way she looked like an angel coming down those stairs.

He managed to convince himself over and over again that she was off-limits as Chris's little sister. It wasn't worth losing a friendship over an unrequited crush.

Natalie had ended up dating Brad for most of high school. And as soon as she graduated, she was off to the city.

And Shane had ended up marrying MaryLou, whose farm was next to his family's.

At the age of eighteen, he hadn't been planning on marriage and a child so soon, but Wyatt had come along as a surprise. And all the pieces of the puzzle that was his life seemed to fit together perfectly as soon as he looked down at the sweet little bundle in his arms, a golden wedding ring gleaming on his finger as he reached out to stroke that downy cheek, while Lou smiled up at him from the hospital bed.

He was happy helping his parents with the farm and living in the caretaker's cottage with his fun-loving wife and baby Wyatt. When their second little blessing, Rumor, arrived they began plans to build a new, bigger house on the farm for their growing family.

Life had been too filled with busy happiness to think about any alternate routes he might have taken. It had all felt like fate, right up until the night of Lou's accident.

Suddenly, he'd been nearing the end of his twenties, with a ten-year-old and a baby, and a tiny house that somehow still managed to feel empty.

In the three years since, he'd learned a lot about himself and what he was capable of. He'd learned that Trinity Falls was a town full of caring people who wanted to help, though he didn't like taking charity in any form. And he'd grown closer with his parents than he had ever been before.

Seeing Cricket today was a reminder that the story of his life wasn't over yet. Though he still couldn't get involved with his best friend's sister, something about seeing her made him feel alive again - like the snow was melting, and spring flowers were budding underground, ready to unfurl.

"Grandma's house," Rumor sang out from the backseat.

He pulled up next to the great big Victorian farmhouse and saw that his mom already had the manger scene set up out front. A light dusting of snow made it seem clean and new, even though his dad had made it back when he was a kid, and they repainted the wooden figures every couple of years.

But Grandma was clearly waiting for Wyatt and Rumor to help her with the lights and pine trimmings.

Christmas was a big deal on Cassidy Farm, and he was grateful that his parents hadn't slowed that down on his account. Rumor would be in ecstasy helping with the preparations. And Wyatt would really enjoy it too, even if he played it cool.

"Hey," his mom yelled from the wraparound porch. "There's my helper."

Rumor was squeaking and wiggling before he could even get her out of the truck.

When he set her down on the gravel drive, she dashed through the snow, up the front steps, and into her grandma's waiting arms.

Alice Cassidy was short and round, with a bun of chestnut hair streaked with silver, and strong arms that could hug you so hard to her soft bosom it took all your troubles away. She smelled like gingerbread, laughed like a waterfall, and without exception, everyone who knew her loved her.

She led Rumor into the house and glanced back, looking surprised and pleased to see Shane following.

"You have a few minutes to say hi to your dad?" she asked.

"Sure do," he told her. "And if you need anything around the house."

He didn't say out loud that he knew she couldn't rely on his dad to reach the high cabinets for her right now.

"Never offer an old woman a hand around the house," she laughed. "You'll find yourself snowed under in no time."

She was hardly old. But he knew better than to argue with her.

"It's already snowing, Grandma," Rumor squeaked.

"So it is, my girl," she said. "And it makes the whole farm look like a Christmas decoration, doesn't it?"

He followed after them, soaking in the happy, familiar sound of his family.

5

SHANE

Shane didn't follow his mother's admonition to sit and relax until after he'd rehung the family room curtains she'd washed and ironed, and used the old-fashioned key to bleed all the radiators.

On his way back to the kitchen, he refreshed the stack of holiday children's books Rumor was reading with her Grandpa.

"Thank you, Daddy," Rumor said, grabbing her favorite Tasha Tudor picture-book right out of his hands.

"If he keeps this up, I'm liable to get knee replacements every winter," his father said. "*Ha*."

"Oh, Joe," his mom laughed. "Now come on over, Shane. Sit down and let me spoil you just a little."

That was an offer no one could refuse.

He pulled up a stool to the freestanding wooden island and she ladled him out a mug of hot cider.

"Did you eat lunch?" she asked him, gazing right into his eyes so he couldn't lie.

"I'm fine, Mom," he said, shaking his head.

"That's what I thought," she said, marching off to drag

her step stool to the buffet for a bowl. "You need to take better care of yourself. You can't run the farm if you're falling over from exhaustion."

He watched her scoop homemade stew from the big crockpot, his stomach suddenly rumbling to life.

"So, what brings you inside to sit down?" his mom asked, sliding the bowl across the island to him as she cut to the chase, in her usual way.

There was no point trying to keep anything from her. And he found he wanted to talk it out anyway.

"I saw Cricket in town today," he told her. "Natalie Bell."

He paused for a bite of the heavenly stew, mostly so he could see her reaction before saying more

"Chris's little sister," she mused. "She always did have a crush on you."

He gulped and the stew went down a little wrong, leaving him spluttering.

"Oh, surely you knew," his mother laughed. "The way she followed you around, like you made the sun rise and set?"

"She just wanted to be with her brother," he said, recovering a little. "Those two were really close."

"I see," his mother said, as if to say *I don't see, but I'll humor you.* "How's she doing? It's very sad about her Nana. You know Natalie left her life in the city to care for her, and the poor thing only held on a few months after that."

"But she's still here," Shane said, recognizing his dreamy tone too late.

"Well, everyone loves Trinity Falls," his mother said. "And her Nana loved it even more than most. Wouldn't it be nice if she decided to stick around?"

"She was trying to get a job at Jolly Beans when I bumped into her," he said.

That wasn't entirely true. He hadn't exactly bumped into her by chance. He had been planning to take Rumor to the little shop she called the "nut store" to buy penny candies and ask if she could use the bathroom there. But he had seen Cricket in the window of Jolly Beans, and he hadn't been able to resist heading to the café instead.

"She knocked the lady down and all the food went on the floor," Rumor piped up. "The man yelled at her."

The little scamp was paying attention.

"Yeah, she bumped into Holly, who happened to be carrying two giant trays," Shane explained. "Pete yelled at her to get out."

"Oh, Pete," his mom sighed, shaking her head.

"I should probably call him and ask him to hire her," Shane realized out loud. "He owes me one."

"No, she's going to be my nanny," Rumor scolded him.

"Is that so?" his mom asked, trying and failing to hide her big smile behind her hand.

"I felt bad for her," he said, which also wasn't really the whole truth. "She needs a job, and since I can't find help with the horses, I figured I might as well hire her to help with the kids instead. It would free me up to do more farm tasks myself if Rumor had an everyday sitter. And you've got your hands full with Dad."

"What's that supposed to mean?" his father spluttered.

"It means I've got to keep a hawk eye on you, mister," his mom said. "Don't pretend I didn't catch you trying to go down to get the mail yourself yesterday."

"You can't coddle me forever, woman," his dad grumbled.

"Eight days," she told him. "Eight days, and you didn't even have your walker."

Shane met Rumor's eyes and winked.

She grinned back at him.

Her grandparents loved to argue, but it was just for show. In reality, they loved each other so hard it was almost embarrassing.

"So, are you going to call Pete?" his mother asked.

"No," he said, thinking about it. "I don't like the way he talked to her."

"Remember that when she's working for you," his mom said wisely.

"What's that supposed to mean?" he said.

"I know you like to do things for yourself," she replied. "Your own way. And you come by it honestly."

"Hey," his dad pretended to protest.

"But if you hire her to help you, you have to let her help," his mom went on. "And she won't always do everything exactly the way you would."

"Got it, Mom," he said, feeling a little irritated. If the woman was working for him, why wouldn't she do things his way?

"That's my boy," she said, reaching out to pat his hand and giving him a twinkly smile. "Now make that stew disappear. There's an apple crumble in the oven."

"I can't stay for dessert," he told her. "I've got to get back to the horses. Thanks for watching Rumor."

"We're always glad to have her," his mom said. "And she's going to be a terrific help. What do you say to making cookies once the crumble's done, Rumor?"

"Yes," the little one confirmed happily. "Cookies."

Shane finished his stew and carried his dishes to the sink.

"I'll get those," his mom said. "Let me walk you out."

She took his arm and they headed to the front door

together. She took a moment to slip on a sweater, then they stepped out onto the porch.

"It really is beautiful, isn't it?" she asked him as they looked out over the farm. "Like a snow globe."

The snow was sticking just enough to frost the greenery. Big flakes still drifted down, though it had slowed a little.

"Yeah," he agreed.

She said it every time it snowed, but she meant it. And she was right. The farm had belonged to the Cassidy family for generations. The sight of it spread out before them always moved him. He found it beautiful in every season.

"I wanted to say something without the little pitcher listening in," she said after a moment.

"I figured," he said, nodding.

"I think it's wonderful you're hiring Natalie," she said. "And I meant what I said in there, don't mess this up. She's a good girl, and I think she can offer understanding to your kids that few other people could."

"Her parents died in a car crash," he remembered out loud.

"Her daddy was in school with your Aunt Tru," she said. "She always said Jeb Bell was quiet and reserved. When he married that girl from the city, everyone was surprised."

"Was Cricket's mom quiet too?" he asked.

"Not even a little bit," his mom said, shaking her head and smiling. "She used to come into town with the music in her car turned up so loud that your daddy joked it would shatter the windows in the shops. Couldn't have been more opposite to her husband."

"I wonder what they saw in each other," he said.

"She was on the wild side, but she didn't have a mean bone in her body," his mom told him. "And it must have been hard for her to go from the city to a farm town like that, so she certainly loved him. I remember seeing her here and there with Chris and baby Natalie. She was always sweet with the kids."

"Chris remembers her," Shane said thoughtfully. "He said once that she used to sing all the time."

"She loved music," his mother agreed. "They were on their way to a concert in the city when it happened. Carla was watching the kids. And of course, she just kept them after that. They were lucky to have her."

"They know," Shane said. "I could tell Cricket was hurting today."

"So be kind," his mom said, giving him a pat on the shoulder. "You two have plenty in common."

He turned and studied her through narrowed eyes.

Did she know about the crush he secretly harbored for Cricket? Was she trying to give him her blessing?

Though she often encouraged him to get out in the world and enjoy himself, his mother had never once pressured him to date or try to find someone new. Every busybody in Trinity Falls seemed to be mentally setting him up, some of them even vocally trying to do so.

But his mom understood the loyalty he still felt to Lou.

Besides, between the kids and the farm, he wasn't ready to share another moment of his time with anyone else. Rumor and Wyatt were entitled to whatever pieces of him were left at the end of the long days.

One of which was about to get even longer if he didn't get out of here.

"I'll be nice to her, Mom," he said, wrapping his arm around her shoulders and giving her a little squeeze. "She's Chris's little sister. If I'm not nice, he'll kick my butt."

It might be a couple of months, since Chris was

currently stationed at a base in the middle of the Pacific, but it would definitely happen.

His mom chuckled and squeezed him back, then let him go so he could walk through the snowy yard to his truck.

When he pulled out of his spot, he turned and saw that she had waited outside to wave goodbye to him from the porch, like she always did.

Waving back, he thought to himself with satisfaction that Alice Cassidy was the only woman he needed in his life.

But maybe that wasn't exactly the whole truth either.

6

NATALIE

Natalie's alarm went off at six-thirty. The room was still cast in darkness, and she was disoriented for a minute.

She wasn't in her apartment.

Blinking, she recognized the shapes of the furnishings and the laundry scent of the sheets and realized she was in her old room at Nana's house.

For one bright moment, she wondered what Nana was making for breakfast.

Then reality finally folded in on her again, and she remembered why she was here, and that she was alone in the house.

And then she remembered why she'd set the alarm in the first place.

"I'll make breakfast for Rumor," she told herself with forced cheer.

Dragging herself out of bed wasn't easy, but Shane had said *first thing,* and that probably meant before her usual wake up time around nine.

She woke up the rest of the way as she showered, and

then stood in a robe in her room for a few minutes, trying to decide what to wear.

She finally chose a pair of faded jeans and a navy-blue button-down corduroy shirt. Her favorite brown cowgirl boots from high school were the obvious choice to complete the outfit.

She pulled her hair back and decided against make-up for the second day in a row. Childcare was hands-on stuff.

And besides, Shane had seen her that way yesterday. She wouldn't want him to think she was trying to make herself look pretty for him today.

She tried not to think about whether she actually wanted him to find her pretty. It would be awful to have such thoughts about a man who had lost the mother of his children, and love of his life.

Glancing around the room to make sure she wasn't forgetting anything, she was relieved to spot her sheet of notes on the nightstand. She had googled a list of questions last night that she wanted to ask him before he headed out.

She grabbed it and reviewed it again, making a mental note of the most important ones, in case he was in a rush, or there was chaos in the house when she got there. Then she folded it and slipped it into her pocket.

Hopefully, they could exchange numbers, and she could ask him the rest before tomorrow if he didn't have time to talk with her today.

She locked up the house and headed down to Nana's ancient Nissan hatchback.

The tiny gray car was almost twenty years old, and needed to be babied a little. Nana had always warmed it up for five to ten minutes before driving, so Natalie did the same.

If Nana would have treated herself to a newer car

without the burden of providing for her grandchildren during her retirement, she never said a word about it.

Instead, she kept the interior clean and cozy, and they festooned the rear bumper and eventually the whole back end with the stickers she got from the charities that came calling.

Nana would never say no to an earnest pitch. She liked to say the stickers on the car in the driveway were like the old hobo markings, letting other young volunteers know it was safe to come by and ask for a signature to save the forest, or a few dollars for the school.

Nana would have been sad to know they were finally breaking ground for the big highway, tearing down sections of trees, and even moving a whole neighborhood of homes down by the woods.

The announcement had been the headline in the local paper barely two weeks after Nana passed. Natalie would never be glad she was gone, but part of her was glad she never had to see that.

"The end of an era," Natalie said to herself as she pulled carefully out of the driveway and headed toward Cassidy farm, thinking about the changes on the way.

The highway had been in planning stages for a quarter century, with various possible routes floated.

No town wanted to lose its charm by having a highway bisect it. And many towns were more powerful than Trinity Falls - powerful enough to block their routes from the map.

At least the route they finally landed on curved around the western border of the town rather than slicing through it. The paper made sure to note that the highway would cut the commute to Philadelphia in half, and improve everyone's property values.

Whether or not that was true remained to be seen. But she knew at least one person had banked on the possibility.

A man from the city had bought up Gladys Livingston's farm on Route 1, and then he'd bought land from the Millers and the Pruitts on either side.

He was the one who was apparently hiring so many workers that no one else could find help this year.

If it means I got a job, then I can't complain, she reminded herself. After all, if Shane had found ready farmhands, he wouldn't need someone else to be with his kids.

The idea was a sad one. As she drove the winding lanes of Trinity Falls toward the farm, she decided that she would do her best to treat the kids as if they were her own. If he couldn't be with them himself, she'd be the next best thing.

The sun was climbing above the tall trees, casting the lake in pinky gold colors as she drove past. The grass along the lake was tipped in lacy frost. The holidays were definitely coming.

With Chris away on duty and Nana gone, she had no idea what she was going to do. Even the ladies from town would have to find another woman's home to host the holiday parties and book club meetings.

She pushed the worries away as the big wooden sign painted with apples and horses welcomed her to Cassidy Farm.

She smiled and turned down the gravel driveway. The hatchback bumped hard in a big pothole, and then slid a little when she hit the brakes.

Heart pounding, she took her foot off the gas and eased down the drive slowly, hitting a few more big bumps and plenty of smaller ones.

Her Nana had always driven them here, but she didn't remember it ever being so bumpy.

She drove past the orchards, then the fields where blueberries grew in the summers under netting to keep the birds out, and down the dirt road that led to the line for pick-your-own, the hayride station, and the outdoor nursery.

The big, octagonal barn was home to the Christmas-All-Year-Long shop and the bakery with pies and country home decor. The small fresh grocery stand, and then the pens of farm animals visited on school trips were on her right, and the paddock where even the littlest kids could learn to ride was on the left.

After that, the dirt road narrowed, and a small sign noted that she was entering private property.

She could just see the big Victorian farmhouse where the Cassidy kids had grown up, set back on the right, the Christmas tree farm covering the hill behind it.

Continuing straight, she passed the big red barn on her left and the stone caretaker's cottage on her right, and finally, Shane's new home came into view.

At first, she thought she must have remembered his directions wrong. The house beyond the barn looked like another Victorian, with white clapboard siding and black shutters, just like his parents' house.

But as she pulled closer, she saw the tiny details, like perfectly even front steps, and smooth, modern glass windows, that gave away that his home wasn't as old as it seemed.

The fact that he had built something that fit into the farm's old-fashioned setting, rather than a more modern-looking mansion, said a lot. Nana always said that quality cost. Natalie couldn't imagine what Shane had spent for gingerbread trim and bric-a-brac instead of a flat face of whisper-thin stucco.

The Cassidys were farmers. There was no way Shane had the money to pay someone to do that kind of work.

Which meant he must have done it himself.

She suddenly pictured him out here, carefully measuring and cutting each shake. Even in her imagination, his patience was steadying.

She scanned the front of the house as she pulled Nana's humble hatchback up beside his shiny truck.

That kind of woodwork needed regular painting. Natalie knew first-hand from the big painting job she had taken on every five years or so on Nana's bungalow. If it hadn't been a one-floor home, it would have cost a fortune to hire someone. As far as she could see, this house was three full stories. And harsh Pennsylvania winters meant Shane wouldn't be able to skimp on paint quality.

"Cricket," Rumor yelled from the porch. "You came."

"Of course I did," Natalie laughed, her breath pluming in the cold air. "I told your Daddy I would. I can't believe you're awake."

"It's *late*," Rumor wailed.

"It's not quite eight," Natalie said. "That's pretty early, I think."

Was it?

Rumor was fully dressed, and her hair was damp and combed.

"Glad you could join us," Shane said, stepping out onto the porch. "Your alarm didn't go off?"

"Uh, you said first thing," she said. "It's not even eight."

"Are you joking?" he asked, his blue eyes narrowed.

She shook her head slowly.

"Maybe this is first thing in the city," he said, an irritated look on his face. "But out here we get to work before the crack of dawn."

"Which is?" she asked.

"I'd like you here by six," he said. "That way you can wake Rumor up and get her and Wyatt fed and ready for school while I'm getting the first of the morning chores out of the way."

Good heavens.

"I understand," she heard herself say. "I will be here tomorrow by six."

Somehow.

"Good," he said gruffly. "Rumor needs to get to pre-school now, and I'm very late starting chores. So why don't you get her packed up and over to the church."

"Of course," Natalie told him. "What about Wyatt?"

"He was on the bus at six thirty," Shane said. "You'll meet him this afternoon."

She bit her lip and nodded, feeling too horrible to speak. She had really messed up, and he was clearly unhappy with her.

She jogged up the steps as fast as she could and bent down to greet Rumor.

"I'm sorry I was late, Rumor," she said. "Your daddy is absolutely right, farm first-thing and city first-thing are very different. But now I understand. Let's find your bag and get it packed for pre-school."

Rumor gave her a sweet smile and grabbed her hand, dragging her into the house.

She glanced over her shoulder to make sure Shane had heard her apology too.

But he was already jogging down the stairs, the stiff set of his shoulders telling her he was still unhappy.

What a way to start.

7

NATALIE

Natalie let Rumor lead her inside.

She was still feeling shaken by Shane's admonishment. She remembered him as such a kind and patient boy.

Time changes people, Nana used to say.

And Shane had been through a lot.

"Oh," she said, as she stepped in and looked around the foyer.

The space had the same high ceilings and woodwork an older house would have had.

It was also filled to the brim with boxes.

"That's all our stuff," Rumor said, looking at the boxes.

"You guys just moved in here, huh?" Natalie asked. "I'll bet you're excited to get unpacked so you can have all your books and toys."

"I have my blocks," Rumor told her, with a serious expression. "Grandma helped me carry them, so they wouldn't have to go in a box."

"That was very smart," Natalie told her. "Moving is hard,

and sometimes it takes longer than you think it will to get unpacked."

Rumor blinked up at her, as if she didn't understand.

"Let's get you ready for school," Natalie said. "Where's your backpack?"

Rumor took off down the hall toward the back of the house, where the hall opened into a massive kitchen.

It felt like the classic Victorian kitchen, but three times the size, with all the woodwork and cabinets painted in creamy white. Skylights let in the pale morning light and big windows revealed the farm outside.

A purple backpack sat in the center of the marble topped island.

"That's yours?" Natalie asked.

"Yeah," Rumor told her. "I like purple."

"Me too," Natalie said. "Do you have a snack in there?"

"Apples and cheese stick," Rumor announced.

"Perfect," Natalie told her. "Do you have a sweater in there?"

"Nope," Rumor said.

"Okay, I think a sweater is a good idea," Natalie told her. "What else do you normally pack?"

Rumor shrugged.

"Run and grab a sweater," Natalie said. "We'll head out after that."

Natalie picked up the backpack and walked back down the hall to the front door as Rumor's footsteps disappeared up the stairs.

There were so many boxes in the entry that it seemed like they must contain most of the family's possessions.

Having them in the entryway was a danger. She and Chris had been junior volunteer firefighters in high school. She knew anything that could potentially block or partially block a means of egress was a danger. And these boxes were paper and flammable themselves.

Rumor thundered down the stairs with a lumpy green woolen sweater.

"Got it," she said, triumphantly brandishing the sweater.

"That's a very cozy looking sweater," Natalie told her. "Did someone make it for you?"

"Mama made it for Wyatt," Rumor said proudly. "But now he's too big."

"How lovely," Natalie said. "I'll bet you can feel her love hugging you every time you put it on."

Rumor smiled and reached for her backpack.

Natalie surrendered it and watched the little one cram the sweater inside, resisting the impulse to do it for her.

When the backpack was safely zipped up, she helped Rumor put on her coat and they headed out into the cold morning.

"Is that your car, Cricket?" Rumor asked, her eyes wide.

Natalie opened her mouth and closed it again. She wasn't going to apologize to a four-year-old about her perfectly serviceable vehicle.

"It has *stickers*," Rumor cried rapturously.

Natalie smiled and followed her little charge out to the car.

"Where's my seat?" Rumor asked, when she opened the back door.

"Oh, no," Natalie breathed.

Where to find the carseat and how to install it were questions written on the list that was still folded in her pocket.

"Does your daddy keep a spare seat for you?" she asked Rumor as calmly as she could.

"My old one is in the garage," Rumor said. "I still fit in it."

Natalie pictured a baby seat and bit her lip, but they didn't have a choice. She followed Rumor into the garage and was relieved to see a good-sized car seat with a few stains.

"Let's see if Nana's car has latches," Natalie said, lifting the unwieldy thing.

"Who is Nana?" Rumor asked.

"She was my grandma," Natalie said. "My car used to belong to her. I still think of it as her car. Isn't that funny?"

Rumor shrugged and they headed back to the car.

Natalie placed the seat on the ground and ran her hands along the crease in the backseat.

"Hot diggity-dog," she exclaimed happily when she felt the metal latches. "We're in business."

Rumor exploded into a fit of giggles, and Natalie smiled while she lifted the carseat in, buckled it with the belt, and shoved it down until she felt a good click.

Grabbing it with both hands, she shook it as hard as she could.

It held firmly and didn't move overly. It would be good enough to get the little one to preschool if she couldn't find her dad on the way out.

Once she dropped Rumor off, she'd stop by the firehouse to get the guys to check it for her. She remembered the bi-annual car-seat check days well enough to get the seat in firmly. But not well enough to be sure she had made every adjustment ideally.

"Okay, time to get in," she told Rumor.

"*Hot diggity-dog,*" Rumor yelled as she scrambled in. "*Hot diggity-dog.*"

"We might be a little late today," Natalie told her. "But safety is our first priority, right?"

"Hot diggity-dog," Rumor agreed.

They headed slowly out the gravel driveway. Natalie looked around for Shane, but she didn't see him or his car.

After a few minutes, she pulled out on Knowlton Road and headed for the village.

"Can we hear songs?" Rumor asked.

"Sure, but it has to be my favorite station," Natalie teased. "And they're only playing holiday music right now."

"Christmas carols," Rumor crowed.

Natalie turned on the radio and *Jingle Bell Rock* greeted them. Rumor began singing along immediately.

Natalie let herself enjoy the sweet little voice crooning along to one of her favorites.

Is this what it would have been like if she'd decided to marry Brad Williams and settle down after high school?

She had never regretted her decision to follow her dreams. It would not have been fair to Brad or herself for her to leave such an important stone unturned.

But she was twenty-seven now, and had no prospects and no right to start looking, until she figured out what she was doing with her own life.

At this rate, I'll be forty before I start dating again.

Rumor just had time to finish singing *Jingle Bell Rock* and then *The First Noel* with Natalie singing along too when they turned into town and then made a right to head for the church.

"Trinity Nursery Day School," Rumor called out, pretending to read the wooden sign next to the drop off area.

Kids ahead in line were piling out of pick-up trucks,

SUVs, and minivans. Natalie felt like she was dropping Rumor off in a miniature car.

When they pulled up, she realized in frustration that she had the car set on the wrong side.

And the door the teacher was going to try and open was the one that stuck.

She scrambled out and got Rumor out on her own side, then walked her behind the car.

She bent to say goodbye, but Rumor had already disappeared into the press of little bodies in colorful coats.

"Oh, hello there," a kind-looking young woman with dark hair and a pretty smile said to her. "I'm Miss Cabrera. You must be Rumor's... aunt?"

"I'm her new nanny," Natalie said. "It's nice to meet you, Miss Cabrera."

"It might be easier for next time if you can put her car seat on the other side," Miss Cabrera said politely.

"That door doesn't open very easily," Natalie said quietly, willing herself not to apologize for her finances. She was living within her means, there should be no shame in that.

"Should I jiggle the handle?" Miss Cabrera guessed.

"And pull really hard," Natalie said gratefully.

"Not a problem, "Miss Cabrera told her. "We had one just like it growing up. They don't make them like this one anymore, the new ones are all built to break. Personally, I would drive it into the ground."

"That's definitely the plan," Natalie said, grinning.

"See you at eleven thirty," Miss Cabrera said, giving her a wave before turning to the next car.

Natalie drove off, thinking that it definitely could have gone worse, and feeling hopeful about the rest of the day.

8

NATALIE

Natalie waited in the parking lot while the chief of the Trinity Falls Fire Department personally installed Rumor's car seat on the right side.

She had offered to do it herself and have him check, but he insisted. She figured he was just glad to see her outside of Nana's funeral.

"How's your brother?" Ashton Beck yelled out to her as he emerged from the firehouse.

"He's good," she guessed. "He doesn't call home much these days, but last we spoke, he was working hard."

"Good man," Ashton said, nodding. "What are you doing here? Are you going to volunteer in the big leagues now?"

"I hadn't thought about it," she admitted.

He was right, she qualified now to volunteer as a regular firefighter, not just a junior apprentice.

"Community College kids don't volunteer as much as they used to," Ashton said. "And they can't come running any time of day either."

"Neither can I, these days," she admitted.

"You got kids now?" he asked, glancing from the carseat to her hand, no doubt looking for a ring.

"No," she said. "I'm working as a nanny, though."

"Who for?" he asked.

"Shane Cassidy," she told him, wondering if Shane would have wanted her to share, when she had just started, and he was already mad at her.

"Nice," Ashton said, frowning.

"What's that supposed to mean?" she laughed.

"I dunno," Ashton said, smiling back. "I guess he's just been kind of a control freak since he lost Lou. Don't let him push you around."

"Oh, he wouldn't," she said immediately, feeling a little surprised that she was so quick to automatically defend the man who had scolded her this morning. "He's a very nice man, and a good father."

"I see," Ashton said, winking.

Natalie spluttered and searched for something to say that wouldn't dig her in deeper.

Of course, Ashton was only teasing, right?

"Looks good now, Nat," the chief said, puffing up the slight hill to her. "You had it in there just fine on the other side, by the way. But I'm always glad to take a look if you ever need to take it out and want to put it back in again."

"Thank you so much, Chief," she said sincerely. "I'm very grateful."

"Don't suppose you have any time for volunteering these days?" he asked hopefully. "We're short on crew, though I guess with the little one, you can't be at my beck and call."

"No pun intended," Ashton said, winking at her again.

"Very funny, Beck," the chief said good-naturedly. "Anyway, if you ever want to get involved, you know where to find us, Nat."

"Thanks, Chief," she said, heading down to her car.

She still had two hours before it would be time to pick Rumor up from school.

Shane hadn't said what he wanted her to do during the break. She cringed inwardly, thinking about what he might say if she guessed wrong.

The Co-op grocery store was right across from the municipal parking lot. She decided to pop over and grab some things to cook up for lunch. After all, Nana always said the way to a man's heart was through his stomach.

If Shane had been working double-time on chores since she left, it would be nice to offer him something better than cold cuts for his lunch.

She headed in and grabbed a rotisserie chicken, some veggies, and all she needed to make a homemade crust. There was no telling what, if anything, Shane kept around the house. If the movies were accurate, single dads ordered a lot of pizza.

She made a mental note to take stock of his cupboards as soon as she got back.

After a nice chat with Marge at check-out, who had been a friend of her Nana's, she walked back to the car.

The radio started up with the car and she kept it on, humming and singing along to the music all the way back to Cassidy farm.

~

AN HOUR LATER, she was wandering around Shane's kitchen while her veggies simmered, feeling a restored faith in humanity.

Unlike the single dads in the movies, Shane had plenty of supplies in his kitchen. Not only the tools and appliances that might have been left over from married life, but also a full component of well-organized spices, baking ingredients, a crisper full of veggies along with the baskets of fruit she'd seen on the counter this morning.

There was meat in the freezer too, but she had no idea what his plans were for the groceries he already had. What he wanted her to prepare and feed to the kids was another unanswered question on her list.

Once her inventory was complete, she set about taking apart the chicken. Normally, she would cook one from scratch, but time was short today.

She got the meat and veggies for the pot pie filling ready, and left it on the stove top with the lid sealed tight to keep it warm.

Then she whipped up a quick crust, rolled it out, and stuck it in the fridge, figuring that Rumor would enjoy helping her build the pies.

Once she was done, she fixed herself a glass of cold water and leaned back on the counter to drink it. The alarm on her phone went off just as she finished.

The ride back to pick up Rumor went off without a hitch. And now that the seat was in the right spot, and Miss Cabrera knew about the tricky door, she was able to pick up Rumor without incident.

"She had a busy day," Miss Cabrera said as Rumor scrambled in. "Her teacher, Mrs. O'Toole, wants to meet with her dad one day soon to talk about goals."

"Okay," Natalie replied, uncertain whether that was good or bad. "I'll let him know."

"Thanks," Miss Cabrera said.

"Bye-bye," Rumor told the teacher.

"How was your day?" Natalie asked as they pulled out, figuring she would steal a move out of Nana's playbook.

"I dunno," Rumor said quietly.

Natalie had met the child less than twenty-four hours ago, and she still knew that was out of character.

"What was the best part of the day?" she tried asking.

"I played outside," Rumor said.

"With the other kids?" Natalie asked.

"Yeah," Rumor said happily.

"And what was the worst part of your day?" Natalie asked.

"We had to go in," Rumor said. "We couldn't stay out."

"You had to go in before you were ready," Natalie said. "That's so frustrating. How did it make you feel?"

"Mad," Rumor yelled.

Natalie thought of her time as a camp counselor, and how some of the kids just needed to blow off some steam once in a while.

"Let it out," Natalie told her. "Roar."

"Roar?" Rumor said uncertainly.

"Yes," Natalie said. "Roar it out."

Rumor tilted her little head back and let out an impressive roar.

Then she started laughing.

"That was a good one," Natalie told her. "Feel any better?"

But Rumor was having a giggle fit now, roaring a little between giggles.

Natalie smiled to herself and turned on the radio. Before long, they were home and happy.

"Put away your backpack, and then meet me in the kitchen," Natalie told her.

"I don't put away my backpack," Rumor said, throwing it on the foyer floor next to the wall of boxes and turning to run to the kitchen. "My daddy does it."

"Are you too little?" Natalie asked her.

Her little shoulders stiffened as if her pride had been wounded.

"I'm not too little," Rumor said, spinning around. "My daddy puts my things away."

"But I think you're big enough to do it yourself," Natalie said. "Open it up and let's see what we've got going on in there."

Rumor frowned, but she followed instructions.

"Your snack bag should go in the kitchen," Natalie told her. "And you can take out your sweater in case you want to wear it tonight."

Rumor trotted to the kitchen with her snack bag and came back for the sweater, shrugging it on, instead of putting it away.

Since it was a little chilly in the house, Natalie didn't argue.

"Great job," she told Rumor. "Now you just have to zip up the backpack and put it where it goes."

Rumor crouched to carefully zip up the bag, then trundled up the stairs with it.

Natalie headed to the kitchen and pulled the pie crust out of the fridge.

By the time she had everything ready to go, Rumor was back.

"What's *that*?" she asked, looking at the dough.

"I'm making chicken pot pies for lunch," Natalie told her. "But I could use some help."

"I'll help," Rumor said regally.

"Excellent," Natalie said. "Should we have some music on while we cook?"

Rumor nodded hard, so Natalie turned on the radio that sat in the corner near the sink.

White Christmas began to play, and they got down to business.

"You've helped out in the kitchen before," Natalie said, when Rumor started by dragging a step stool over to the sink to wash her hands.

"I help Grandma," she said.

"What about Wyatt?" Natalie asked. "Does he help Grandma too?"

Natalie shrugged.

"Or does he help more with farm stuff?" Natalie guessed.

"Yeah," Rumor said.

She got down and dried her hands on the towel hanging from the stove.

"Great job," Natalie told her. "Let's get started."

They worked happily, singing along with the radio as they cut and shaped the crusts. After the pies were in the oven, they did a quick clean up and Rumor played with her blocks on the living room table.

The front door opened just as Natalie was taking the pies out of the oven.

"Daddy," Rumor yelled, thundering toward him as he stepped inside.

"Something smells good," his voice boomed.

Natalie headed toward the open arch to greet him.

He had lifted Rumor into his arms and was spinning around with her while she shrieked with glee.

It felt like a private family moment, but somehow, she couldn't get her feet to move.

When was the last time she just let go and felt pure happiness like that?

9

SHANE

Shane held Rumor close and drank in the sounds of her happy laughter as he swung her around.

Moments like this made it all worthwhile, and helped him feel like he was getting some things right. He might not be able to be with Rumor as much as he wanted, but if she was glad to see him when he came home, that had to be good enough.

And it was also a sign that Cricket was doing a good job with her.

He glanced up and caught her peeking at them from the arch of the kitchen, a dreamy look in her eyes.

"Hey, Cricket," he said, gently placing Rumor on her feet. "How was your morning?"

"It was productive," she told him politely. "How was yours?"

"Productive," he echoed and grinned at her.

"Rumor and I made chicken pot pies for lunch," she told him. "We were hoping you might join us."

"That's what smells so good," he said. "Yes, absolutely. I'll just wash up."

He had already kicked off his boots on the porch. Now he jogged upstairs to shuck off his work clothes.

He thought about just putting on clean clothes, but caring for sixteen horses on his own this morning had left him muddy and sweaty, in spite of the cold. So, he hopped in the shower and took two minutes under the hot, steamy water to clean himself up.

When he got out and pulled on clean jeans and a t-shirt, he felt much better. He jogged back down the stairs, the incredible scent of lunch making his belly rumble.

Now that the morning's work was done, he was feeling more like himself. Which gave him the headspace to think about how he had spoken to Cricket this morning.

For all that he'd promised his mother and himself that he would treat her kindly, he'd done just the opposite.

Yet she had obviously pulled the morning together anyway. And now she had made him lunch, something he never would have expected her to do.

Determined to do better as a boss, he headed into the kitchen and was greeted with a sweet domestic scene.

Lunch was set out on the big table. Three pot pies, each set on one of the nice blue china plates got his attention right away. A pitcher of what looked like iced tea rested at the center of the table.

Cricket was showing Rumor how to set the silverware, their bodies leaned together as they talked quietly.

He leaned on the threshold for a moment, taking it in.

Cricket looked up after a moment, as if she sensed his presence, and he swore her cheeks went a little pink.

"It looks amazing," he said, enjoying the way she smiled at his praise.

"We figured you would be hungry, right Rumor?" she said, turning her attention to his happy daughter.

"We made sweet tea," Rumor announced.

"That sounds great," he declared, heading over to the table.

He decided to pull Cricket's chair out for her, and got a kick out of the look of pleased surprise on her face.

Cricket poured them each a glass of tea and Rumor took a big sip right away.

"Mmm-mm," she said, her adorable dimples showing. Sometimes she looked so much like her mother that it almost hurt.

"We did a good job?" Cricket asked her.

"We did a great job," Rumor crowed.

Shane closed his eyes for a second to offer up his thanks for the meal, and then grabbed his knife and fork and dug right in. The fragrance of the pie was savory and delicate at the same time.

"Did you make this crust from scratch?" he asked.

"Of course," Cricket told him. "It's much nicer that way. Besides, the pre-made ones cost a fortune."

"A woman who knows the value of a dollar," he said, nodding to her as he took a bite.

The flavors exploded in his mouth, reminding him of childhood and the chicken and dumpling soup his mom used to make on snowy days.

"So good," he crooned.

"Mm," Rumor agreed.

They ate in friendly silence for a few minutes, and he noticed that Rumor cleaned her plate. Normally she lost interest after a few bites and had to be cajoled to eat more.

Maybe if I had time to fix her something better than peanut butter and jelly...

He glanced at Cricket again, glad that he had hired her,

and even more glad that she hadn't quit this morning when he spoke sharply to her.

"Can I play with my blocks now?" Rumor asked.

"Sure, kiddo," he told her. "I'm going to sit with Cricket for a minute."

Rumor slipped out of her chair and dashed back to the low table in the living room, where she had started constructing a building of some kind.

"She's a really special girl," Cricket said, smiling fondly after her.

"That she is," he agreed.

"Her teacher mentioned having you in to talk about goals?" she offered uncertainly.

He sighed.

"I wasn't sure if that was good or bad," she said.

"It's probably not good," he told her, running a hand through his still-damp hair. "She's got high energy."

"Is that a bad thing?" Cricket asked, leaning forward.

"Not to me," Shane told her honestly. "And I suspect it might not bother anyone else, if she were a boy. But people have expectations for girls, and she doesn't fit the mold."

"She's *four*," Cricket said. "What kind of mold could there possibly be for a four-year-old?"

The fire in her eyes melted something in his heart.

"Agreed," he said. "Anyway, I'll get in touch with the teacher. Hopefully, I can get it worked out."

"I could come too," Cricket offered. "If you wanted. Since I'm her caregiver for part of the day now."

He glanced up at her and saw the serious expression on her face.

She was not Chris Bell's cute little sister anymore. She was a grown woman who was ready to be fiercely protective of his child.

"I'd like that," he told her, feeling oddly like he had a lump in his throat.

He grabbed his glass and finished off the cold, sweet tea.

It was good to have a real meal in the middle of the day, nicer than he would have thought.

"I guess I should get back to work," he told her at last, placing his glass back down. "Why don't you let me clean up, since you cooked?"

"Not a chance," she told him. "You have a lot to do. I'll bet you're still making up for the morning you missed."

"Hey, about that," he said, standing. "I should have told you yesterday what time I needed you. That's on me. I hope I didn't ruin your morning."

"Not at all," she said, smiling as she rose and helped him collect the plates and cups. "I should have asked what you meant when you said first thing. That's my fault."

"You didn't grow up on a farm," he chuckled.

"I know, I know," she laughed. "I'm soft. I grew up in the village."

"Well, you're doing a great job here," he told her as he started the warm water going in the sink.

"Thank you," she told him. "But I'm not doing the job I could be doing. I've got a list of questions for you. I know you need to get back to work, but maybe you could look them over tonight?"

"Of course," he said, watching her use a fridge magnet to hold the folded piece of paper in place. "I'd be glad to."

"You doing okay, Rumor?" she called, glancing at the girl through the open arch to the living room.

"Great," Rumor squeaked from the living room. "I'm building a barn."

"Well, when I get done cleaning up, I want to have a look

at it," Cricket told her. "It has to pass inspection before we let any elephants in."

Rumor giggled, and he busied himself washing the dishes to hide his goofy grin. She really was good with Rumor. This was going to work out just fine.

"At least let me dry," she scolded him, grabbing for a plate, a towel in her other hand.

He surrendered and offered it to her.

Their hands brushed a little as she took the plate.

A whisper of awareness slid down his spine, as if the gentle touch of her soft hand had awakened something in him.

He hurried through the rest of the dishes, being very careful not to let their hands touch again as he handed them to her.

Before long, the kitchen was sparkling clean, and there was nothing to do but bundle up and head back to work.

"What time does Wyatt get home?" Cricket called to him from her place on the floor by the coffee table, next to Rumor.

"Two thirty," he told her. "Don't let it hurt your feelings if he heads straight for his room. He's got a lot of homework these days."

Not that the kid was doing *that* much homework, based on his grades. But Shane didn't want Cricket to feel bad when Wyatt disappeared, like he did every day.

She turned her attention back to Rumor's barn, making an elephant noise that had Rumor howling with laughter.

Shane headed out to the porch for his boots, wishing he had more help on the farm, so he could stick around and share that joy.

10

NATALIE

Natalie watched as Rumor finished carefully stacking up all her blocks by size and shape in their special chest.

For a kid who didn't want to put away her own backpack, she was extremely conscientious with her blocks.

"You organized them all so beautifully," she complimented the little one.

Rumor's face broke into a radiant smile.

"I love my blocks," she said. "We don't want them to get lost or stepped on."

That definitely sounded like something an adult had said to her. And she had clearly listened.

"You're exactly right," Natalie told her. "Hey, I think we have about an hour before your brother comes home, and I have an idea about what we could do. Do you want to hear it?"

"Yes," Rumor said.

"Should we try to unpack a few things?" Natalie asked.

She expected the little one to get excited.

Instead, a worried look appeared on her little face.

"Daddy says everything is too busy right now to unpack," Rumor said sadly.

"He's been very busy without enough workers, hasn't he?" Natalie asked. "If we take care of the unpacking, then he won't have to worry about it, right?"

Rumor nodded hard enough that her curls bounced a little.

"Okay. Let's start with your stuff," Natalie said. "Can you show me where your room is?"

Rumor took off up the stairs and Natalie followed. When they reached the first landing, Rumor headed for the room at the front of the house.

Natalie trailed her into a beautiful, sun-drenched space. Two windows overlooked the front lawn. The one on the side had a window-seat flanked by bookshelves.

The floors were wide wood planks, painted pale green. A fluffy green rug on top looked almost like fresh spring grass. And Rumor had a pretty white bed with a snuggly horse toy on the pillow and a wooden dresser.

But Natalie was surprised to see that there wasn't another thing in the room. No other stuffed animals, no rocking horse, no easel, no stacks of puzzles and games, none of the things that made a little kid's room fun to hang out in. Even the bookshelves were empty.

"Your room is really cool," she told Rumor, plastering a big smile on her face. "I can't wait to see it with your stuff in it. Let's go grab a box."

The work went by quickly, with Rumor having a pretty clear idea where all of her stuff belonged.

An hour later, they stepped back to look at the room.

A stack of empty cardboard boxes sat beside the bed, but other than that, things looked so much nicer.

A nice pile of stuffed animals had found a home in a wicker trunk by the bedside. Rumor had set out some cute horse figures on her dresser. And the bookshelves were stacked with puzzles, games, and an impressive collection of picture books.

Natalie had even hung up Rumor's costume collection in the closet, since she couldn't think of another spot for the many superhero and princess outfits.

"What do you think?" she asked.

"It looks good," Rumor said, flopping down on the bed. "I want a snack."

"Good idea," Natalie told her. "And your brother will be home soon. Do you think he'll be hungry?"

Rumor shrugged.

"Come on, let's go see what you have for snacking on," Natalie said. "We can carry the empty boxes down too."

Natalie grabbed most of the boxes, leaving the smaller one that had held the figurines for Rumor to carry. They headed down the stairs with their respective burdens, passing the now slightly smaller forest of still-packed boxes in the foyer.

Though most of them were clearly marked, Natalie had made the mistake of opening one that had no indication what was inside, because it was between two that were labeled *Rumor*.

While Rumor organized her puzzles on a shelf, Natalie had removed the first item. It felt like something in a frame, and it was wrapped in newspaper.

She had been unprepared to find a close-up of photo of Shane and his wife.

MaryLou Webb gazed into the camera, her dark brown eyes filled with joy and just a tiny sparkle of mischief. Chestnut curls, like Rumor's, cascaded down her back, and her cheeks had those same dimples that showed up when the little girl was really happy.

Beside her, Shane laughed, his chin tilted up, eyes closed.

Natalie's heart ached as she thought about the pain he must feel now that she was gone.

She had quickly covered the photo with newspaper before Rumor noticed what she was doing, and brought it back downstairs with the other boxes.

She would definitely be very careful in the future not to open anything unless it was labeled with the kids' names, or as something that wasn't private.

They had just reached the kitchen when the front door banged open.

She glanced back down the foyer, but the boxes blocked her view.

"Hey, Wyatt," she called out. "I'm Natalie.'

There was a masculine grunting sound that might have been acknowledgement, and then a flash of dark hair before his feet thudded on the staircase.

"Maybe he doesn't like the idea of having a sitter, since he's a teenager now," she told Rumor.

"Wyatt always goes right upstairs," Rumor said, opening the fridge.

Everyone kept saying that, but Natalie had thought it was an exaggeration. Surely, the kid should at least want to say hi and grab something to eat before disappearing.

"Does he want us to go visit him in his room?" she asked Rumor.

Rumor shook her little head hard enough that her curls bounced.

"I have an idea," Natalie told her. "Let's make him a snack, too. Then we have a reason to go say hi."

"Okay," Rumor said.

They looked around the kitchen a bit. There were apples, and a couple of ancient looking granola bars.

"What do you usually have for a snack?" Natalie asked.

"My grandma makes my snacks," Rumor said.

Natalie nodded. No wonder they didn't have much here, if Rumor was used to spending her afternoons at her grandparents' house.

"Did your grandma make this?" she asked, picking up a loaf of what looked like homemade bread.

"Yes," Rumor said.

"Should we use it to make cinnamon toast?" Natalie asked. "We can make hot chocolate to go with it."

"Yes," Rumor said excitedly.

They prepared the simple snack in record time. The hot chocolate was the kind from the envelopes, with tiny marshmallows, just like she'd loved as a kid. Natalie used a skillet to toast the bread so it would have a little crispiness to it. And so Rumor could feel like a real cook on her step stool with an apron and spatula as Natalie carefully guided her.

"Let's cut them into triangles," she suggested.

"Why?" Rumor asked.

"To make them look fancy, of course," Natalie told her.

Rumor giggled, and used the plastic toddler knife Natalie handed her to carefully cut the toast. It would be a little more torn and smushed than if an adult had done it, but Rumor was old enough to learn.

Natalie rummaged around the mostly-empty cupboards until she found a tea set with fancy china cups on a nice tray. It must have been carried over by hand, and not trusted to ride in a box.

"Perfect," she said, carefully pulling them down.

"Hot chocolate goes in mugs," Rumor told her.

"But this is fancier," Natalie said.

Rumor nodded, like that made perfect sense.

Finally, the whole tray was ready, with cinnamon toast triangles, three delicate cups, and a teapot of hot chocolate.

Rumor led the way upstairs to her brother's room, knocking on one of the two doors that faced the side of the house.

"What?" he said from inside.

Rumor looked immediately to Natalie, as if to say *I told you so.*

"We brought you a snack," Natalie said, in a firm, clear voice.

"Come in," he said after a few seconds.

Rumor opened the door and Natalie stepped in first, carrying the tray.

She was glad to see that he had a desk in his room, at least. There was also a bed and dresser, a stack of books on the floor by the bed, and very little else.

Wyatt sat behind the desk, gazing at her curiously. His dark, floppy hair and handsome face were the spitting image of his father. But he had his mother's soulful brown eyes.

"Can we put this on the desk?" she asked him.

"Sure," he said, moving his notebook and pencil to the side. "Cinnamon toast?"

"Rumor made it herself," Natalie said, nodding.

Rumor sat on the edge of his bed, which was close enough to the desk to use it as a table.

Natalie sat down beside her.

"Good job, Rumor," Wyatt said.

Rumor grinned at him happily.

Natalie grabbed the teapot.

"Uh, I don't really like tea," Wyatt said, looking a little worried that she might be offended.

"This is actually hot chocolate," Natalie told him. "Rumor and I just thought it would be fun to celebrate me getting to meet you finally, so we tried to make the snack a little fancy. I'll bet everyone says it, but you look a lot like your dad."

"Mostly they say I have my mom's eyes," he said, grabbing a piece of toast.

She wondered how he felt about that, but didn't want to push.

"Whoa, it's really good," he said. "You didn't use the toaster."

"How did you know?" Rumor asked, looking amazed.

"Our toaster doesn't toast things evenly," he said with a shrug. "Everything's always partly burned and partly cold."

"We used the skillet," Natalie said, impressed that a kid his age would pay enough attention to his toast to appreciate it.

"Crispy," he said, grabbing another piece. "The skillet really sears in the butter."

"Do you like to cook?" she asked him, handing him a cup of hot chocolate.

He glanced at her with a strange expression, almost as if she had caught him doing something he shouldn't.

He shrugged.

"I love to cook," she told him. "If you're willing to help sometime, I'd be really grateful."

"Sure, I'd help," he allowed, taking a big swig of hot chocolate.

His eyes lit up.

"Why is this so good?" he asked.

"I used a dash of cinnamon and a pinch of salt," she said.

"Epic," he said, downing it in one more swallow.

Rumor hopped off the bed to grab a piece of toast.

"How was school?" Natalie asked Wyatt.

"I dunno," he said. "Boring."

"I remember that feeling," she said, nodding, and hoping he would extrapolate.

Instead, he poured a cup of hot chocolate for his little sister.

"Careful with it," he told her gently. "You're in my room."

"Thank you," Rumor told him with a big smile as she took it.

He tousled her hair and smiled back.

Natalie smiled too. He was a good big brother. That was important.

"I guess I should get back to my homework," he said.

"Of course," Natalie told him. "Come down if you want when you're done. We're going to figure out something fun to do until your dad gets back."

"Bye, Wyatt," Rumor said as she left, carrying her teacup with exaggerated care.

11

SHANE

Shane kicked off his muddy boots and stepped into the foyer and at the end of a long, long day.

The sun set so early in December, and he swore it made him feel even more tired at five than he was in the summertime working later.

The first thing he noticed was that the house smelled good, like cinnamon, and a bit like the pot pie Cricket and Rumor had made earlier.

The second thing he noticed was that the stacks of boxes weren't as tall as before. They had been organized somewhat, so he could see all the way to the kitchen more easily from the front door.

And he thought that somehow, there weren't as many as before.

"We're back here," Cricket called out cheerfully.

He shrugged off his jacket and hung it on the hook, then headed down the hallway to the kitchen, feeling excited at the end of the day instead of just exhausted for a change.

While it was unlikely that Cricket had cooked for them twice in one day, at least things would be neat and tidy, and there might even be enough of those pot pies for leftovers for dinner.

Christmas music was playing on the radio as he stepped into the kitchen, where he was assaulted with an unwelcome sight.

Five or six empty cardboard boxes were spread across the floor, and the counters were covered in stacks of plates, mugs, pots and pans and other kitchen things. Lou's favorite Christmas kitchen flour sack towels, the ones he hadn't had the heart to get out in years, were already hanging from the oven handle.

"Hi, Daddy," Rumor squeaked.

He glanced over to see that she was scrambling around the big kitchen table, sorting through about a thousand ancient metal cookie cutters that had belonged to Lou's mom.

"What are you doing?" he demanded, though it was obvious.

What he should have asked was, *Why are you doing this?*

"We know you're very busy on the farm," Cricket said. "We thought we could help out with the unpacking."

"This isn't a help," he spluttered. "I didn't ask you to go through our things. I didn't ask you to make a mess."

"I'll stay until the kitchen is organized," she said quickly. "You don't have to pay me extra."

"It's not about paying you," he said, exasperated. "This is my house. These are my things. You can't just come in here and take over everything."

"I'm sorry," she said. "I didn't mean to overstep."

"But you *did* overstep," he said angrily.

Why could nothing ever go just right? She was supposed to be making his life easier, not harder. Now, instead of relaxing with the kids, he was going to have to undo whatever she had done and completely organize the kitchen.

"You can't yell at her," Rumor piped up, reminding him of what he had promised his mother.

He sighed and ran a hand through his hair.

"I'll get out of your way," Cricket said brightly, moving from the kitchen toward the hall. "Please leave it just like this. I'll box it all back up in the morning, exactly the way it was when I found it."

"Cricket, you don't have to go home," Rumor said.

"I'll see you tomorrow, Rumor," Cricket called out over her shoulder. "Have a good night, Wyatt."

Wyatt?

Shane turned slowly around the room and spotted his son, out of his room for once, sitting on the floor in the middle of organizing a stack of colorful mixing bowls.

Before his eyes, Wyatt's relaxed expression closed as if someone had pulled the curtains shut.

Wyatt stood and turned off the radio, then headed for the hallway. A moment later, Shane heard his feet on the stairs.

He and Rumor were left alone in unhappy silence - a feeling he was far too familiar with.

He had messed things up.

Jogging to the front door, he could already hear that he was too late to fix it. Cricket's car was starting up loudly.

By the time he got out to the porch, the little hatchback was bumping away up the drive, and sliding a little on the gravel in a way that made him clench his fists with worry. If there was ice, that thing would be no good at all.

He watched her taillights until they disappeared, then headed back to the kitchen to find Rumor looking despondently at the cookie cutters.

"You made her leave," Rumor said accusingly.

It broke his heart a little. Rumor was always generous with him, even when he lost his patience.

"I'm sorry," he said sincerely, noticing the note Cricket had affixed to the fridge on his way over to comfort Rumor.

He grabbed it and shoved it in his pocket.

"She won't come back," Rumor said sadly.

"She'll come back," he told Rumor, patting his lap to encourage her to scramble up for a hug.

She just looked at him for a moment and his heart froze.

Then she slid off her seat and came to him, letting herself be lifted and held close, like when she was a baby.

"I'm so sorry, baby," he told her, drinking in her sweet scent and warm weight. "I'll fix it, I promise."

I just don't know how.

～

THEY MADE it through the night together.

As he had hoped, there were leftover pot pies, carefully wrapped in foil in the fridge. He and Rumor heated them up and even lured Wyatt out of his room for a few minutes to eat at the dining room table, since the one in the kitchen was covered in cookie cutters.

The dining room was very nice. He had almost forgotten it existed as anything but a place to store more boxes.

"We've never eaten in here before," Wyatt broke his usual silence to observe.

"Next time, we can have a fire," Shane offered. "Maybe you can help me with it?"

Wyatt shrugged and turned his attention back to his pot pie, stabbing a chunk of chicken.

"I wonder how she made the roux," he said so quietly Shane thought he might be talking to himself.

"The what, son?" Shane asked. The word sounded familiar, like maybe it got thrown around on Lou's beloved cooking shows.

"Nothing," Wyatt said. "It's good, that's all."

"We made it," Rumor said happily.

"You did a great job," Wyatt told her.

Shane's heart warmed. Whatever might be going on with Wyatt these days, he was still sweet to his little sister. As far as Shane was concerned, that meant his son's character was solid - he was just working through the usual trials of adolescence.

They finished their meal in relative silence. Then Wyatt headed back up to his room while Shane took Rumor up for her bath and bedtime routine.

But before they got to her room, she stopped and faced him.

"Daddy, we unpacked my room," Rumor told him, standing protectively in front of the door.

"I'm sure it looks great," he told her, his heart breaking a little.

How had he become the kind of guy whose four-year-old was worried that he wouldn't like the way her toys were unpacked?

She opened the door slowly, her little cheeks dimpling as she did, like she couldn't contain her own glee.

The room had been transformed. Rumor's horses were on the dresser, her beloved books were on the shelf, and the trunk of stuffed animals looked right at home beside her bed.

"This is amazing," he sang out, moving around the room to look at each area.

Rumor followed him, clapping her hands with delight.

When he had made a thorough inspection of the room, they picked out a fresh pair of pajamas for her, and headed to the bathroom so she could soak in the clawfoot tub.

It wasn't until he had tucked his damp, clean daughter into bed and read her the usual two stories, that he headed to his own room at last.

He laid out his own pajama pants and took a hot shower, then came back into the room to get ready for bed.

But when he went to throw his jeans in the laundry basket, he spotted a piece of paper sticking out.

Cricket's note...

He slipped it out and sat on the edge of the bed to read it.

Penned in Cricket's careful handwriting were a dozen or so really thoughtful questions about how to care for his kids and his home.

He pictured her alone in her Nana's house last night, thinking hard about what his kids might need, and writing these questions at the old kitchen table, and his heart gave a painful lurch for the third time in a day.

"You messed up," he said to himself.

In the note, she asked about what time he wanted her each day, what to feed the kids for each meal, and snacks. She asked about a carseat for Rumor, and it hit him that he hadn't even helped her install one. She asked if he wanted her to prepare his dinner, and if so, what he liked to eat and whether he wanted her to shop for him.

And she asked for his cell number, which he hadn't realized until just this moment he hadn't given her. And she gave him hers.

There were more questions, but they all blurred in front of his eyes.

He needed to call her and apologize, *now*. His behavior had been unforgivable, but he hoped she would forgive him anyway, for Rumor's sake, and for Wyatt's.

But when he glanced at the clock, he thought she was probably asleep after her long day.

He thought about texting, but it seemed like a coward's way.

He knew he was running the risk that she would call in the morning to quit before he had a chance to tell her he was sorry, but he had to bet on her spirit.

The fierce, determined Cricket Bell he had known growing up might be outwardly polite, but she would never back down from a challenge, and she definitely wouldn't break a promise to a little kid.

And before she left, she had told Rumor she would see her tomorrow.

He went to bed, determined to apologize in person in the morning. And he fell asleep while he was still trying to find the right words that would convince her he meant it, that would convince her to stay.

12

NATALIE

Natalie awoke with the golden light of the early morning casting a romantic glow over the room.

Suddenly, the golden light in the room hit her and she realized that it was morning. *Real* morning, not the five in the morning time her phone alarm had been set for.

Why hadn't it gone off?

Sitting up quickly, she grabbed her phone where it was plugged in next to the bed.

A black screen stared back at her. It was dead.

"Howie Linck," she sighed, falling back onto her pillows.

The real estate agent had told her the house was still on the original, old-fashioned electrical system, and some of it wasn't up to the current standard. If she wanted to sell, she had to get rid of the knob and tube wiring and replace it with the newer, safer stuff.

She had called in three electricians. Two had quoted her high enough that she could have gotten an associate's degree at Trinity Falls Community College, maybe even finished off with a bachelors at Penn State for the same price.

The third was Howie Linck.

Howie was getting up there in age. He had lowered his shingle and taken a job with a local company so as to save his bad back. But he remembered when her Nana read to his grandkids at the library as a volunteer, and so his number had been stuck on the fridge as *electrician - reasonable* in Nana's loopy handwriting.

When Natalie called him, Howie offered to take on her job in his off-hours with the help of his nephew. The work would take a while to get done that way, but his quote was a third of what the others wanted, and she could pay as she went instead of emptying Nana's meager bank account all at once.

But Howie sometimes showed up unexpectedly, and sometimes not at all.

And he didn't always tell her when he was deactivating an outlet or a breaker.

She'd already lost a fridge full of groceries last month.

"I guess this month, I'm losing my job," she murmured to herself, sitting up again and feeling numb.

She had fallen into bed last night, her eyes swollen from crying with fury over how stupid Shane Cassidy had spoken to her about his silly dishes.

But at least he hadn't fired her.

Now she was late.

Again.

Hopelessly, unforgivably late.

Again.

She contemplated plugging her phone into another outlet and sending him an *I quit* text as soon as she had enough juice.

But she didn't have his number, and she wouldn't have done that anyway. It seemed cowardly.

She was just going to have to put on her big girl pants and go face the music. Even if this was the end, she had told Rumor she would see her today.

And Natalie would never, ever lie to a little kid.

Especially not that one. Rumor was special.

She hauled herself out of bed and into the bathroom to do a slap-dash version of her morning routine.

She was brushing her teeth, but she wasn't yet showered or dressed when the doorbell rang.

She looked around, as if someone might help her.

But she was as alone in the house as she had been before.

Whoever it was, she had to get rid of them fast, so she could finish getting ready and get to Shane's house.

She spit out her toothpaste and jogged out of the bathroom, sticking her feet into a pair of Nana's pink fluffy slippers on her way to the door.

She was in such a hurry that she didn't even look through the peephole, like Nana had always taught her to do.

So, she was completely stunned when she opened the door to see Shane Cassidy standing on the other side, his hand up like he was about to ring the bell again.

13

SHANE

Shane alternated between gripping the wheel too hard and tapping it impatiently as he drove from the pre-school drop-off toward Cricket's Nana's house in the village.

He still had no idea what he was going to say to her.

He was disappointed that she hadn't shown up this morning, even to tell him she quit. He deserved that, but Rumor didn't.

On the other hand, he had been such a jerk to Cricket that he understood. All of this was on him, not on her.

He couldn't even imagine how Chris would react when Cricket told him what happened. He hated the idea of losing his best friend in all this.

But the more his thoughts continued, the more he was surprised to find that he was more worried about losing Cricket.

She'd spent *one day* in his house, and he already missed having her there. Rumor was more at peace with all that attention. Heck, Wyatt had even been out of his room.

"I will fix this," he told himself. "I will fix it somehow."

He was sure he had failed his kids many, many times since becoming a single dad. But this one felt like the worst. It wasn't a small mistake, a passing hiccup.

It was clear that having Cricket in their lives would have a ripple effect that could make things better for a long time.

He prayed that she would give him another chance.

He pulled up in front of her house and saw that her deathtrap of a car was in the driveway, so she was home.

He still hadn't come up with anything good to tell her, but he hopped out of his truck and jogged up to the porch, figuring it would be better to say anything at all than to let another minute pass without apologizing.

He stabbed the bell with an impatient finger.

After a moment, he heard footsteps and then the door opened for him.

A woman alone should check the peephole, he thought to himself. But he wasn't there to give advice.

And then all thought went out of his mind, and he could barely advise himself how to draw breath.

Cricket stood, gazing up at him, her lips slightly parted in surprise.

Her dark hair was still sleep-tangled, and it hung down around her shoulders. She wore a pink tank top that clung to her curves, and a pair of fuzzy pajama pants with alternating candy canes and Rudolph faces on them. A pair of pink fluffy slippers peeked out underneath.

She was equal parts ridiculous and adorable.

Did grown women really wear silly pajamas? Her get-up looked like something Rumor would pick out.

But it looks very different on Cricket...

"I'm sorry," she said suddenly, before he could decide where to look.

Definitely not at anything below her chin or above her collection of candy canes and reindeer heads.

"The agent says I have to have the house rewired to sell it. And the contractor keeps deactivating things without telling me. My phone died in the night because the outlet wasn't working, and the alarm didn't go off—"

"They didn't tell you what they were deactivating?" Shane asked, angry on her behalf. "Who is your electrician?"

"It's Howie Linck," she said. "But he's doing it as a favor to me, after hours."

He resisted the impulse to roll his eyes. Barely.

Howie Linck had been a casual drinker in his younger days, but as he got older, he started to treat it more like a full-time job, which left less and less time for his actual job. If she was lucky, the rewiring would take him years to finish. If she wasn't so lucky, he might set the whole place on fire.

But she was looking at him with her chin tilted up defiantly, as if daring him to say a word against her choice of contractor.

He let out a breath slowly, promising himself to think about this later. He absolutely couldn't afford to hurt her pride right now. And the only reason someone would choose Howie Linck was if they couldn't afford a decent operation.

A solution occurred to him, and he let it out before he had time to change his mind.

"I understand," he said gruffly. "If you still want to work for me, pack up what you need for the week. You can take the guest room on my third floor. That way we don't have to worry about your alarm. The rooster can just wake you up like it does the rest of us."

Her face softened with wonder for a moment, then she buttoned her lip and tilted that chin up again.

"Don't be proud, Cricket," he said softly. "You'll be doing me a favor. I'd like to know you'll be there in the morning."

She was wavering, and he didn't think she was going to say yes to his face.

"I'll wait out here," he told her. "Take your time."

He headed back onto the porch and sat down on the swing overlooking Park Avenue.

He remembered sitting on this swing a million times with Chris, first talking about cartoons and video games, and then later about girls and future plans.

Sitting here, he could almost believe that no time had passed since he was a goofy teenager hanging out with his best friend, waiting for Nana Bell to bring out a fresh batch of cookies with Cricket at their heels trying to snatch the biggest one.

But of course, Chris was in the military, stationed at an airfield in Hawaii, and Nana Bell was gone.

There was no one left but this grown-up, tired, short-tempered version of himself.

And kind-hearted, confounding, Cricket Bell, still at his heels, but so different than before.

It might not be possible to recreate the past, but maybe there was a future that was a little brighter than the present. It was something to work for.

He was lost in thought when he heard the front door open again.

Cricket came out, her hair smoothed and tamed into a ponytail now, a modest blouse and pair of jeans in place of the funny pajamas, and cowgirl boots instead of fuzzy slippers.

She was carrying a backpack, a reusable Co-op tote, and a guitar case.

"That's all?" he asked without thinking.

"I travel light," she said, shrugging. "Besides, this is only temporary."

Something in him was riled by that *only temporary* even though of course it was only temporary. It wouldn't be the busy season on the farm forever, and living in his attic probably wasn't on her list of life goals.

"Come on," he said, taking her bags and heading to his truck.

"I should drive, or I won't have my car," she told him.

"That car isn't safe on my driveway, especially in wintertime," he told her. "I'd rather you use one of my trucks."

He waited for her to argue.

"I guess it's safer for the kids," she allowed thoughtfully. "Let me just get Rumor's carseat out."

"I've got it," he told her. "Least I can do."

They moved to the car together, but she let him take the lead.

He gave it a subtle shake and was impressed to find it was installed very firmly.

"What?" she asked.

"You did this yourself?" he asked. "It took me a lot of practice to get it right."

"I was a volunteer firefighter," she reminded him. "So, I know how to do it, because I worked the free-carseat-check days. But I had the chief redo this for me just to be sure, since it's been a while for me."

"That was very thoughtful of you," he told her, glad to hear she wasn't cutting any corners.

"Keeping the kids safe is my whole job," she said, as if it were the most obvious thing in the world.

They headed back to his car.

He fought the instinct to open her door for her. *This isn't a date, Cassidy,* he reminded himself.

Instead, he busied himself throwing the carseat and her bags into the bed of the truck while she got into the passenger seat.

"It's so neat," she said when he joined her in the cab.

"You think all men are slobs?" he teased.

"No, but you have kids," she laughed.

"You think all kids are slobs?" he chuckled.

"Yes," she said decidedly. "Which means you make an effort to keep this truck nice. I wasn't sure if the house was clean because you just got there, or because you keep it that way."

"We didn't just get there," he told her.

She nodded and her eyes went to the storefronts they were passing.

"It's been a little crazy," he admitted, glad she wasn't looking at him. It made it easier to talk. "And I just... haven't found the time to unpack. It was nice of you to help out with that - really, really nice."

"You didn't seem to feel that way last night," she said.

Her voice was neutral and soft - not angry or sarcastic.

"It's been a long time since there's been another grown-up in the house," he admitted. "I guess being the only adult is encouraging my inner control freak. But I want you to know how sorry I am for last night. I am determined to do better."

He had practiced apologizing and begging her to come back so many times last night.

And now she was coming with him. And she had agreed to pack her bags and follow him out even before she got the apology she deserved.

"You're right," she said calmly. "It's not good for the kids to hear you talk to me that way. But everyone makes mistakes."

He nodded and kept his eyes on the road, not trusting himself to reply without getting sappy and scaring her away.

The truth of the matter was, it wasn't good for *her* to hear him talk to her that way. She deserved better, much better. And he was very lucky she was in his life.

When the village faded into the countryside, she turned to him.

"Mind if I put on the radio?" she asked.

"Not at all," he told her.

The sound of Rumor's all-Christmas station came on the speakers, where Elvis was wailing for Santa to bring his baby back.

Cricket leaned forward again, he figured to change the station.

Instead, she turned it up and started singing along, so joyfully that he couldn't resist joining her.

14

NATALIE

Natalie was laughing her head off at Shane's rendition of another Elvis Christmas classic as they bumped up the driveway toward the house.

He had been so serious since they saw each other at the café. It was nice to see his playful side come out.

"Sorry about the drive," Shane said. "My dad normally rakes fresh gravel on every couple of years, but he had a double knee replacement, so he's benched for the season."

"Your mom must have her hands full," Natalie guessed, trying to imagine Mr. Cassidy refraining from his farm tasks. Shane's dad had always been big and strong, like his sons - the vision of a hard-working man. She remembered him being perpetually in motion.

"She does," Shane laughed. "Speaking of hands full, I've got a ton to do today. I'll drop you here and leave another truck in the drive with the key on the seat before you have to pick up Rumor."

"Okay," she said, trying not to feel embarrassed about Nana's hatchback. "Thank you."

"My pleasure," he told her. "Don't feel like you need to

cook a hot lunch or anything. Just get unpacked and settled in, okay?"

She smiled and hopped out, grabbing her bags from the back, and giving him a little wave when she reached the porch.

She watched as he pulled out and wondered what he was working on today. Hopefully, whatever it was went well enough that he didn't lose the good mood he was in.

Heading inside was different this time. She knew what to expect. And also, this was now *home*, at least for a little while.

She crossed the foyer to the stairs, admiring the slightly smaller collection of boxes, and headed up.

The stairs to the third floor squeaked a little, so she would have to take them slowly if she wanted to sneak down for a cup of tea on a sleepless night. But they weren't too steep.

She opened the door and stepped into a beautiful, cozy room with sloped ceilings.

A queen-sized bed was tucked against the far wall with a sunny window, and there was a skylight on each slope of the roof, allowing even more soft light in. The wood plank floor had been painted pale gray and a soft rug in blues and greens matched the pretty comforter on the bed.

The whole thing looked so welcoming that she was half-tempted to crawl in and go back to sleep.

But there was no way she could risk sleeping through Rumor's pre-school pick-up. And besides, whether she needed to or not, she was determined to make a nice lunch again.

A small wooden dresser beside the bed turned out to be empty. She was able to fit her clothing and possessions in it.

She had told Shane she packed light, but in reality, she

didn't own all that much. She had cleared out as much of her high school stuff as Nana would allow before heading to New York.

And once she was there, she earned so little and shared such a tiny space with so many roommates, there was no point trying to add to her possessions.

She had a few more pairs of shoes and couple of pretty dresses back at Nana's, but not much more to her name.

Maybe moving out would be easier than trying to give away Nana's stuff while I'm living there...

The thought blindsided her, and she stood in the middle of the room with the empty shopping tote for a moment, wondering why it was so easy to think about living without Nana's things while she was here, and so impossible to think about it while she was there.

Part of it was the difficulty of seeing the house emptied out.

But there was something else, too. Something about having Nana's belongings around made it seem like she might be just in the next room, ready to ask for help with a batch of cookies or a run to the church donation hub.

The sound of a doorbell interrupted her train of thought for the second time that day.

She wondered who it could possibly be. Like most rural residents of Trinity Falls, Shane didn't seem to lock his door during the day, so even if he had forgotten something, he wouldn't be locked out.

Surely, if he was expecting someone, he would have told her.

And it was pretty unlikely to be a solicitor. It was one thing to get people ringing the bell all the time asking for sales or donations when you lived just outside the village. But out here on this long, bumpy drive?

The doorbell rang again, and she hustled down the stairs.

"Coming," she yelled out, uncertain whether anyone would even hear her when she was this far up.

At last, she reached the foyer and opened the front door, panting a little from the rush.

A pretty, blonde woman stood there, holding out a casserole dish that was filled with something greenish and unidentifiable.

"Oh," the woman said, looking very surprised. "Hello."

15

NATALIE

"Hi," Natalie said, smiling as brightly as she could. "I'm Natalie, how can I help you?"

"I'm Amanda," the woman said. "Is Shane here?"

"You just missed him," Natalie said. "He's working now. I was just unpacking."

Amanda's smile froze, and she didn't respond.

"Did... you want to come in?" Natalie offered.

"I'd love to," Amanda said, recovering.

She breezed past Natalie, straight for the kitchen, as if she had been here many times before.

Natalie followed her slowly, hoping it was okay that she had let the woman in. Shane hadn't said not to let anyone come inside. And the kids weren't even home.

Amanda placed the casserole dish on the counter and began tapping away on her cell phone.

Natalie took advantage of the opportunity to surreptitiously check her out.

It was impossible to miss the fact that Amanda's hair was beautifully styled, and that her makeup artfully accentuated her pretty face. On closer inspection, Natalie saw the high-end labels on her yoga pants and jacket, and her flawlessly clean designer sneakers.

There was no way any of those clothes had ever been sweated in. And the driveway out front was probably the roughest terrain the trainers had ever touched.

The outfit was probably worth more than a week of Natalie's pay at any job she'd ever had.

"So, let's get to know each other," Amanda said, looking up suddenly from her phone with a smile so bright it was almost scary. "I'm sure you already knew my name. I've been keeping these guys in home cooked meals for months now."

"That's very kind of you," Natalie said, trying to keep up.

"Now that you're here, I guess I'll be able to free up some time," the woman joked. Her laugh was a little too high-pitched.

Suddenly, it struck Natalie like lightning.

This woman thought Natalie was Shane's live-in girlfriend. She had probably been bringing meals and hoping to snag him for herself, and she now saw Natalie as a romantic rival, swooping in out of nowhere to steal her claim.

Natalie opened her mouth to set the record straight, and a strange thing happened.

A possessive instinct gripped her heart, and she found she couldn't bear to share the truth just yet.

"I'm still finding my way around the kitchen," Natalie said instead.

"I can see that." Amanda scanned the counters covered with items Natalie and the kids had unpacked last night and hadn't been able to put away because of Shane losing his temper.

"We're just in the middle of unpacking," Natalie said lightly. "I'm not normally this disorganized, I promise."

"I hope not," Amanda sniffed, then her face took on a mournful expression. "Shane and the children deserve someone who can put their health and comfort first, after all they've been through."

Natalie nodded noncommittally.

Personally, she didn't think Shane needed a partner at all. He was a very capable man, and he clearly loved Rumor and Wyatt. He just needed a sitter so he could get a little extra work done. But something about the way Amanda was talking made it sound almost like she thought he couldn't keep the kids healthy and comfortable on his own.

"A lot of people around town seem to think we'd be the perfect couple," Amanda went on with a pretend giggle. "So, if you hear any rumors like that don't take them to heart. How long have you two been seeing each other?"

The jig was up. It was one thing to let the woman make the wrong assumption. But Natalie would never outright lie.

"Oh, we're not seeing each other," she admitted.

Amanda blinked at her, and then her smile turned warmer.

"Oh my gosh, how funny," she said. "When you said you were moving in, I just assumed. You must be one of the aunties. The kids must be so excited that you're here. How long are you staying?"

"I'm the new nanny," Natalie told her. "This is temporary. Just while Shane gets through the holidays on the farm."

"I see," Amanda said, straightening up.

She had a smug little closed mouth smile on her face now. It was very different from the confidential warmth she had shared with the person she thought was Shane's family member.

"Did you want me to pass along any message for you?" Natalie offered.

"Please let him know I stopped by," Amanda said crisply. "And let him know this stew is vegetarian, organic, and it has a probiotic boost. It should keep the family going in this cold weather."

"Thank you," Natalie said, trying not to gag at the idea of the so-called *stew* in that dish, and praying Shane would not expect her to eat it. "You obviously went to a lot of trouble to make this. I'm sure he'll appreciate that."

Amanda nodded and headed for the front door.

"Bye now," she called out over her shoulder as she headed outside without even waiting for Natalie to reply.

Natalie followed her to the door and then watched from the window as she hopped into her sporty little car and headed down the driveway fast enough to kick up gravel.

Although Natalie had never been the kind of person to resent the prettiest, wealthiest girls at Trinity Falls High, she found herself feeling like she was in high school all over again - invisible, except to Holly and a few other friends.

Jealousy and resentment shot through her, even as she tried to make herself listen to reason.

Yes, men liked women like Amanda. But who could blame them? Amanda obviously expended quite a bit effort and money to look nice. And she had spent time preparing that ghastly stew, with her heart in exactly the right place. She was trying to express care for someone she was interested in, and his kids. She felt sympathy for the family.

Amanda was under no obligation to be extra nice to Natalie.

And if she cared about him, why shouldn't she get her man?

It's not her fault I had a crush on him when I was a kid,

Natalie scolded herself. *And it's certainly not her fault I'm having a hard time reminding myself not to have a crush on him now.*

She marched back to the kitchen, determined to do better. There should be just enough time to get everything put away before she needed to pick up Rumor.

16

NATALIE

Natalie stepped out onto the porch and looked for her car, forgetting for a moment that she had left it in Nana's driveway.

Instead, an ancient truck was sitting in the spot where she had parked yesterday.

It was a massive thing that looked like it had been built to chase dinosaurs or drag trees down, during a historical time period when those were normal activities.

What must have once been an impressive candy apple red paint job had now faded to the pale color of a half-ripe grocery store tomato.

This was what Shane thought would be safer for her to drive than her Nana's perfectly serviceable hatchback?

She shook her head, but moved down to check it out. He was the boss, so if this was what he wanted, there was no reason she couldn't comply.

"It'll make Nana's car seem new," she said to herself.

Getting in was a challenge. It didn't have a built-in step like a modern truck. But she managed.

Sure enough, he had installed Rumor's spare carseat in the back row. And, as promised, keys were on the seat.

She put them in the ignition and turned.

The engine roared to life with a sound like a dragon, furiously protecting a cache of eggs.

"Good heavens," she murmured, catching her breath.

At least she was used to letting the hatchback warm up. By the sounds of it, this beast needed a minute to calm itself, too.

When the growling rumble had evened out to a purr that seemed to vibrate her fillings, she eased the thing into motion.

She had to admit that it handled itself nicely on the gravel drive, even if the bumps were a little jarring.

By the time she got it out onto the main road, she was feeling slightly more confident.

She didn't see any other cars, so she tested out the brakes and was surprised to find they worked better than she'd expected, though the thing wasn't as responsive as the hatchback.

Figuring it was a long shot, she leaned forward and turned the knob for the radio.

To her surprise, it came to life instantly, playing the last few measures *Carol of the Bells* through the tinny speakers.

"No way," she said to herself, smiling.

"You're listening to WCCR," the announcer said. *"All Christmas music all the time, from November first to New Year's Day."*

Natalie couldn't help smiling. It was the same station she and Rumor had been listening to.

"As you know we're partnering with Robin Hood Jewelers on Fifth and Walnut in Philadelphia," the announcer went on. *"With our help they're going to give away a one-carat diamond*

engagement ring this holiday season. So, keep listening to WCCR to find out how you and your special someone can celebrate this snowy season with some extra ice."

Natalie glanced out over the lake as she passed, and wondered why they had to turn every holiday into a couples' holiday. Or maybe they didn't, and she was just feeling lonely.

"I'm Billy Jay," the deejay said. *"Bing, take it away."*

The sweet strains of *I'll Be Home for Christmas* transported Natalie's heart and got her thinking about her brother, Chris, and how good it would be to see him. But then the song about the Grinch came on, and she pushed all the melancholy feelings aside and drove the rest of the way into town without thinking about anything except that she was excited to see Rumor and hear about her day.

Pulling up in the parking lot, she could see the kids were all outside, playing and having an amazing time with the tricycles and toys.

But one child was hunkered down on the bench, not playing with anyone - a child with a familiar-looking coat.

Don't be Rumor. Don't be Rumor. Don't be Rumor.

As soon as she got a little closer, her heart sank. It was definitely Rumor.

She tried to catch the little one's eye, but Rumor never looked up.

There were signs stating that parents and caregivers had to stay in their cars, but Natalie was sorely tempted to hop out anyway and run to her charge.

At last, the cars moved again and one of the teaching assistants fetched Rumor.

She glanced up at Natalie in the truck and then let her head fall again, her lower lip pouted out.

"Hey there," the assistant said, her dark ponytail moving

over her shoulders she helped Rumor in. "She had kind of a hard day today. Staying still during story time was too challenging, so she had to sit on the bench during outside play. Did Mrs. O'Toole tell you she wants to meet with Rumor's dad?"

"Miss Cabrera let me know," Natalie replied, her mind racing to keep up with what was being said and understand it. "I'll remind him."

"Good," the assistant said. "Gotta keep the line moving now."

She slammed the door shut before Natalie could protest that the assistant was the one who had been keeping *her* there to talk.

She glanced in the rearview mirror before pulling out, only to inadvertently discover that she and Rumor were wearing identical annoyed expressions.

"Are you okay, Rumor?" she asked.

"I was in trouble," Rumor said.

"It was hard to stay still during story time?" Natalie asked.

"It's boring when Mrs. O'Toole reads," Rumor said sadly. "She doesn't even do the voices."

Her phone buzzed before she could even try to figure out what to ask or say to Rumor to help her.

Shane will be home for lunch, she reminded herself. *If I can't cheer her up, he'll know what to do.*

"Hang on, kiddo," she said, pulling the massive truck over to check on the phone.

There was a text message.

SHANE CASSIDY (BOSS):
I'm really sorry, but I won't be back to the house for lunch

today - too much going on.

So, there would be no help from Shane after all.

She held back a sigh and reminded herself that she had dealt with unhappy campers all the time back in high school. She could handle this.

Me:

It's fine. Is it okay if I take Rumor to the park to eat lunch and play?

Shane Cassidy (boss):

That sounds really nice, Cricket. Thank you.

She let out a sigh of relief and tucked the phone in her pocket before looking back to the rearview mirror.

"Hey, Rumor," she said. "I have an idea."

Rumor lifted her chin slowly and met Natalie's eyes in the mirror.

The worried look on that little face broke her heart. No four-year old should feel that way.

"That text was from your daddy," Natalie said. "He can't make it back to the house for lunch, so I asked if it was okay for us to eat our lunch in the park, and then play."

Rumor perked up, her eyes suddenly dancing.

"What did he say?" she whispered.

"He said yes," Natalie told her, unable to hide her smile.

"*Yes,*" Rumor said, grinning right back.

"Should we grab a sandwich at Jolly Beans and head right over?" Natalie asked.

"Yes," Rumor said, beginning a list of all the nice things she wanted to get from Jolly Beans, including ice cream, candy, and root beer, none of which were even on the café's limited menu.

Natalie smiled and let her enjoy her visions of sugarplums while she pulled out and headed into town.

An upbeat jazz version of *Deck the Halls* came on WCCR, and Natalie figured the day was plucking up after all.

17

NATALIE

Natalie helped Rumor out of the truck, placed her on the sidewalk, and held out a hand.

Rumor grabbed it eagerly, and they headed into the café, hand in hand.

The rich scent of coffee welcomed Natalie, and helped offset the sense of embarrassment she felt thinking about her last visit.

It was tempting to just stay away, but she couldn't avoid the best café in Trinity Falls forever, especially when her best friend worked here.

"Hey, guys," Holly called out from behind the counter, where she was pouring a frothy drink.

"Hi Holly," Natalie said as she and Rumor approached. "This is my friend, Rumor."

"Hi," Rumor squeaked, clearly delighted to have been called *my friend*.

"It's nice to meet you, Rumor," Holly said. "I'm Holly. You guys are friends, so you can grab any table you want."

Natalie smiled. The café was self-seating, but Rumor

didn't know that, and she was smiling up at Holly like she hung the stars.

"We were just going to grab a sandwich and a couple of water bottles and eat at the park, since it's not raining," Natalie said.

"Or snowing," Rumor added.

"That sounds amazing," Holly said. "I sure wish I could join you. Why don't you guys grab a table and I'll whip you up my favorite sandwich. You don't have any allergies, do you?"

Rumor shook her head no.

"Lucky girl," Holly said with a wink. "Go relax, and I'll be right over with your stuff all packed up."

They headed to a table by the big front window and Rumor ran right up to point out the snowflakes they had made last time.

"Wow. They look great, don't they?" Natalie asked.

Rumor nodded up and down, her wondering eyes still fixed on the snowflakes.

"Rumor, what would you think about making some Christmas decorations for your new house?" Natalie asked.

"Yes," Rumor said, turning to her excitedly. "I want to do that."

"We'll have to ask your daddy what he thinks," Natalie told her. "But I'll bet we could think of some cool stuff to make."

"Christmas horses," Rumor yelled.

"I don't think I know what those are," Natalie admitted.

"Peanut Butter and Pickles," Rumor said. "They're the Christmas horses."

"Wow," Natalie said. "Do they live on the farm?"

"Yes," Rumor said proudly.

"I'd like to meet them one day," Natalie told her.

Holly came by with a brown bag and two bottles of water.

"Here's your sandwich, ladies," she said. "I threw in some chips."

"Awesome," Natalie said, pulling out her wallet.

"It's on the house," Holly said. "Pete feels bad for yelling at you."

Natalie glanced up to see Pete give her a wave from behind the counter.

"But he wants you to know he wouldn't have hired you anyway," Holly went on.

"Why not?" Natalie asked.

"He says because, and I quote, *I can't have the two of you yukking it up all day*," Holly said, rolling her eyes.

"Yukking it up," Rumor echoed delightedly. "Yukking it up!"

"He's not wrong," Natalie admitted. "I like yukking it up with you."

"Me too," Holly said. "Besides, you clearly got a much better gig."

They both smiled fondly at Rumor for a moment.

"Let's go to the park," Rumor reminded them.

"Right," Natalie said. "We should get going. Please thank Pete for me. Tell him no hard feelings."

"Will do," Holly said, winking again and disappearing back into the thicket of tables.

Natalie took Rumor's hand again and they headed out into the cold afternoon.

After crossing the street, they passed Gabriel's Drugstore, where Natalie's Nana and her friends had sipped floats at the soda fountain back when they were in school.

There were a bunch of other storefronts, but Rumor dragged her up to the real estate office.

To Natalie's surprise and delight, Rumor pressed her little nose against the glass, looking at the Victorian dollhouse decorated for Christmas.

"Wow," she breathed. "Pretty."

"It sure is," Natalie told her, swallowing over a lump in her throat.

The lady behind the glass gave her a little wave. Thankfully it wasn't Natalie's own agent, who would have come out and started grilling her about whether or not the house was empty.

"Hey, Wipeout Girl," said a passing kid holding a skateboard. "Nice."

Wipeout Girl?

She wasn't really sure what that meant, but suspected it had something to do with the incident at Jolly Beans, and wasn't eager to pursue it.

"Ready for the park?" she reminded Rumor.

"Yes," Rumor said, pulling away from the glass.

There was a cut-through in the alleyway between the real estate office and the rug shop, but Natalie kept going, preferring to walk past the ballet school where she had spent so many happy days.

The Arts & Crafts building was just as she remembered it, with a golden ballerina painted on the wooden sign out front.

"This way," she told Rumor.

They walked up to the school, and then took the side path that wound up running the length of the park.

Trinity Falls had several parks, but this one was ideal for pre-school aged kids. It was fenced in, with a ring of shade trees to keep it comfortable in the summertime, and it had safe equipment for little kids to play on.

The sign said *Cassidy Corral*, because the land had been

donated by Ry and Lynn Cassidy, Shane's older cousin and his wife, who owned the house next door. But everyone in town called it the tot lot.

"No one's here," Rumor moaned.

"I'll bet by the time we finish eating our lunch, someone else will come," Natalie guessed.

"Let's find out," Rumor said. "I want chips."

"Okay," Natalie laughed. "Let's put some on our sandwich and eat that first. Then if we're still hungry, we can have more chips for dessert."

Rumor frowned but nodded.

Natalie hid her smile. The child was reasonable.

She opened their water bottles, feeling grateful that it wasn't terribly cold out today. They might shiver a bit in the shade eating lunch, but by the time they moved around a little, they would be fine.

Rumor took a big sip while Natalie unwrapped their sandwiches, opened a pack of chips, and tucked a few under the bread.

"*On* the sandwich?" Rumor asked, delighted.

"Sure," Natalie said. "It makes the sandwich crunchy."

"Yum," Rumor said, taking hers as soon as Natalie held it out.

They ate in friendly silence, Rumor making exaggerated crunching noises with every bite.

Before Natalie was done with her half, a man was approaching the gate with a little boy about Rumor's age.

"See?" she said to Rumor.

Rumor grinned, put down what was left of her sandwich, and rocketed toward the gate to greet the boy.

"Justin," she yelled, her curls bouncing like crazy.

"Natalie Bell?" the man said.

He was under the shade of the big chestnut tree by the

gate and the sun was in her eyes, but when he followed the kids into the center of the park, she saw that it was Cal Cassidy, Shane's older brother, wearing the uniform of the county police.

"Cal," she said happily.

"I didn't realize you were staying in town," he said.

"For now," she said, shrugging. "I'm supposed to be cleaning out Nana's house, but it's not going well so I figured I'd better look for work."

"Is that why you're with Rumor?" he asked.

"Yes," she said. "I'm watching her and Wyatt for your brother, since it sounds like he's overwhelmed at the farm."

"Interesting," Cal said, looking thoughtful.

The kids galloped past, both looking deliriously happy.

"You're a police officer now," she said to Cal. "That's amazing."

"He's the *sheriff*," Justin yelled as they circled the bench.

"Okay, okay," Cal laughed.

"You are?" Natalie asked.

"Interim Sheriff," he said. "Bill Webb retired unexpectedly after his heart issues. He's okay now, but he decided he wanted to spend more time with his family. So, they appointed me to take over until the next election."

"I'm really happy for you," she told him. "And the county is lucky to have you."

"Keeps me out of trouble," he said. "But unfortunately, it means I'm not much use to Shane. And he needs all the help he can get with Dad down for the count."

"What do you mean?" Natalie asked. "I thought your parents retired."

"They did," he laughed. "But you can't keep my dad from the horses. Retirement doesn't mean anything to him when it comes to those animals. But he had a double knee replacement just over a week ago. So this year, he really can't do anything on the farm. And Shane is the only one of the kids that can really pick up the slack. The rest of us are too busy or too far away."

He sounded a little guilty, but she guessed being a new sheriff was pretty time-consuming.

"And someone bought Livingston Farm, and they're hiring anyone with a pulse," Natalie said, remembering what Reggie Webb had been saying to Shane at the café.

"Hey, you're up on the local gossip," Cal said, sounding impressed.

"I heard that at the coffee shop," she laughed. "Why would someone buy all that land and hire all those people?"

"He probably thinks with the highway coming in, it will increase in value," Cal said. "Some people are even wondering if he's got all those guys clearing that land for farming, or if he's got something else in mind."

"Wow," Natalie said.

She and Nana had always worried about the displaced wildlife and the sounds of the roadway. It hadn't occurred to her to worry that the promised bump in property values would displace their human neighbors, too.

There was an explosion of giggles as Justin went down the slide on his belly, head first.

"Justin," his dad called to him. "Be a good example for your cousin, please."

"Backwards," Rumor yelled. "Backwards, backward, *backwards*."

"Frontwards for you, Rumor," Natalie called to her. "Okay?"

But Rumor had already lost interest in the slide and was sprinting for the swings.

"She's a feisty one," Cal said.

"She just needs to get it out," Natalie said, shaking her head. "I wish the pre-school understood that. She's a really good kid."

"She has O'Toole, right?" Cal asked sympathetically.

Natalie nodded.

"Justin is in Miss Cabrera's class," Cal said. "She's the new teacher for the Kindergarten complement. He loves her, even though he's had some struggles with other teachers. Seems like she's really patient with the kids."

Natalie remembered that Miss Cabrera was the one who was working the car line on Natalie's first day. She had seemed so nice.

"Rumor needs that," Natalie said, nodding. "Mostly though, she needs a chance to stretch her legs. I think she's getting in trouble because they expect her to sit still too much. She's only four."

"Justin says Miss Cabrera sets a timer and when it goes off, no matter what they're working on, they stop and have a dance party," Cal chuckled. "So, I guess she's found a way to help them get rid of the excess energy."

"She sounds amazing," Natalie said.

"I haven't met her yet," Cal admitted. "Our admin, Gillian, has a daughter over there, and she brings Justin to me for a quick howdy here before afternoon kindergarten drop-off."

"That's really nice," Natalie said.

"Takes a village, right?" Cal asked, winking. "Speaking of which, I've got to get him back to the station so Gillian can get them to school. I'm glad we swung by here today and got to see you and Rumor."

"Me too," she said, smiling when he clapped her on the shoulder.

"Probably see you again at the farmhouse soon," he said

as he waved for Justin. "I have a feeling my mom will want to spend some time with you."

He was strolling out of the park with Justin by his side before she could ask him what in the world he was talking about.

18

SHANE

Shane stepped onto the porch feeling exhausted and anxious about the meeting he'd scheduled with Mrs. O'Toole.

Mrs. O'Toole had been around the block a few times. Back in the day, she was Shane's pre-school teacher, too.

He remembered being pretty rowdy and hearing his name called out a lot. But as far as he knew, his parents had never been brought in for a meeting.

Whatever was going on with Rumor must be pretty serious.

He was used to worrying more about Wyatt, who was so reserved that it was hard to know what was going on with him. Worrying about his upbeat, energetic daughter was new.

Though he would never have asked her to be there, he was glad Cricket was coming with him. She couldn't do much more than provide moral support, but that meant more to him than she could ever know.

A part of him was worried about that, too. He shouldn't be relying on her already. Her presence shouldn't have this much impact. As hard as he was trying to keep his feelings completely professional, it was already impossible not to think about how well she fit into his life, into all their lives.

He shucked off his boots in the vestibule and stepped inside, bracing himself for Rumor to rocket to him and tackle him with a hug while yelling a mile a minute.

Instead, the house was calm and quiet. It smelled like something was cooking, but whatever it was couldn't hold a candle to the pot pies they had made yesterday.

Don't be a spoiled prince. You didn't hire her to cook, he reminded himself. *It's kind of her to make anything at all.*

He headed back to the kitchen and was stunned to see Rumor curled up on the sofa with a book in the living room on his way past.

"Hey, sweetie," he said, stopping to kiss the top of her head. "What are you reading?"

"It's about dragons having a tea party," she said with a happy smile.

"That sounds awesome," he told her. "Grandma's on her way here to be with you while Cricket and I go run an errand."

"Okay, Daddy, love you," Rumor said, turning back to her book.

He watched her for a moment, stunned. Rumor *never* sat quietly with a book like that.

Cricket really did have a magic touch when it came to his kids.

"Hey, Shane," Cricket said a moment later when he joined her in the kitchen.

She stood at the island with Wyatt, who was mixing something, his expression intent and happy.

"What's cooking?" Shane asked.

"Well, a friend of yours stopped by today," she said, with

a strange expression. "Amanda? She brought you guys a casserole, so we're just heating that up in case you wanted a late lunch before we head out. And then Wyatt and I thought we would make some banana bread, since the bananas were getting brown."

"Oh, no," he groaned.

"Were you saving them for something?" she asked.

"No," he said. "You're welcome to anything you find in the kitchen."

"It's the casserole," Wyatt said to her with a mischievous grin. "Didn't I tell you?"

"It's not very nice of us to laugh at Amanda's casseroles," Shane said, feeling a little bad. "Amanda means well. We shouldn't make Cricket think we're ungrateful people."

"Dad, she *saw* it," Wyatt said. "I'm sure she doesn't want to eat it either."

"Oh, she's not eating that," Shane said definitively. "No one is. We'll order a pizza tonight or something."

"Thank heavens," Cricket said, letting out a sigh of relief so palpable he had to chuckle at her.

"My mom's headed over," he told her. "She'll watch the kids while we're at the school. When we come back, it'll be time to test out the carriage."

"*Yes*," Wyatt said.

"You mean the horse carriage?" Cricket asked, her pretty hazel eyes widening.

"Sure do," Shane said. "I couldn't stop for lunch today because I was halfway through the job of cleaning and prepping the carriage and harnesses. Our family always takes it on a test run before the first weekend of carriage rides on the farm."

"That sounds amazing," Cricket said, suddenly looking down at the bowl his son was stirring.

If he didn't know better, he would think she was feeling... sad?

"Family traditions are the best," she said quietly. "I'm glad you guys have such a special one."

Jiminy Christmas, he had made her think about her Nana. That woman had practically run everything Christmas in Trinity Falls. And now she was gone, and it didn't sound like Chris was liable to be home anytime soon either. He hadn't even made it home for the funeral.

"You *have* to come with us," Wyatt told her with his gentle smile.

Shane could have hugged him.

"Oh, I wouldn't want to get in the way of your family tradition," she demurred.

"You heard the boy," Shane told her enthusiastically, so she would know he meant it. "We won't go without you."

"I would love to come with you," she said, looking up at him, her hazel eyes luminous.

The front door opened, tearing his attention away from her.

"Grandma," Rumor yelled from the living room.

"Are you *reading a book*?" her grandmother asked.

"I don't know how to read, Grandma," Rumor said. "I was looking at the pictures."

"I'll read it to you," her grandmother told her. "Let me just say hi to your dad."

His mom bustled in with a reusable shopping bag that he suspected was full of baked goods.

"Hey, Mom," he said. "You remember Cricket Bell?"

"Of course I do," she said, turning her warm smile to Cricket. "I'm so glad you're here to help with the children. The whole family is very lucky."

Cricket's cheeks went pink, and he wondered if she would be too shy to reply.

"It's my pleasure," she said, smiling back. "They are easy to spend time with."

His mom wrapped an approving arm around her shoulders and gave her a squeeze.

"I know you two need to go," his mom said. "But when you come back, you're having dinner at our place after the carriage ride. Your father is bored. And by the smell of this place, Amanda Luckett has been here and left behind another of her experiments."

"Thanks, Ma," Shane told her, bending over to kiss her cheek. "Let's go, Cricket."

"See you later," Cricket said to his mother and son as they headed down the hallway. "Bye Rumor."

They pulled on their coats and headed out to the porch.

The air was clear, but it smelled like snow again. Shane drew in a deep breath.

"It's going to be okay," Cricket said softly. "Rumor is an amazing kid."

But he couldn't help the way his stomach tightened or the worry that coiled in his heart as they headed to his truck.

19

SHANE

Shane didn't bump into his former pre-school teacher often, but when he did, he normally noticed how much shorter she was than he remembered. And how much older, too.

But tonight, Mrs. O'Toole might as well have been ten feet tall with superpowers. Shane felt dwarfed in her presence as she gestured him to the one chair opposite her desk.

The chair was made for a child. When he sat, assuming he didn't break it, he would have to look up at her.

Not to mention that there was no chair set up for Cricket.

"Miss Bell, isn't it?" Mrs. O'Toole said, glancing over at her.

"Yes," Cricket said. "Nice to meet you."

"I knew your grandmother," Mrs. O'Toole said, not following up with a host of compliments and condolences, as anyone else would have done.

"I'm glad," Cricket told her. "Let me just grab another chair."

"As a matter of fact, our student privacy policy dictates

that I cannot discuss Rumor's schooling with anyone but her parent or guardian," Mrs. O'Toole said.

"I would like her to stay," Shane said. "She is Rumor's caregiver, so she should be part of this conversation."

"Understood," Mrs. O'Toole said, her lips forming a straight line. "But we will be having a frank discussion about your daughter's behavior. If you want to keep family business in the family, now's your chance to take advantage of your right to privacy."

"I choose to waive that right," Shane said carefully, his heart wavering between anger and stomach-dropping fear over what Rumor could have done that would result in this kind of concern about who was here.

Mrs. O'Toole gave a little shrug, as if to say, *On your head be it.*

Cricket grabbed another chair, an adult-sized one, and dragged it over, gesturing that Shane should take it.

She sat in the student chair herself, and he gratefully sat down beside her.

Mrs. O'Toole straightened the stack of papers on her desk, cleared her throat, and fixed Shane with a small smile.

"Let's talk about Rumor," she said. "In spite of her disadvantage, she's a very bright girl. She enjoys art and she's full of energy."

"Excuse me," Cricket said politely. "What is her disadvantage?"

"The loss of her mother, of course," Mrs. O'Toole said.

"I see," Cricket said.

"As I was saying," Mrs. O'Toole went on, "Rumor has promise, but her lack of self-control is making it difficult for her and the other students in my class to get the education they come here for."

"Lack of self-control?" Shane echoed, feeling sick.

"She needs help focusing," Mrs. O'Toole said. "A little support from home might go a long way."

"What do you mean by focusing?" Cricket asked.

Mrs. O'Toole turned to her with a smile that said she thought Cricket was less than bright.

"Here's an example," the teacher said. "Today, I read out loud to the children. Rumor began fidgeting after just a few minutes, and by the end, she was in the back of the classroom, walking around. A four-year old should be able to sit and listen to a story. She'll need that skill for kindergarten next year."

"I'm so sorry," Shane began, "I'll talk to her—"

"Wait," Cricket said, lifting her hand up as if to silence him. "Wait just a minute. I want to make sure I understand."

"Of course, Miss Bell," Mrs. O'Toole said with another fake smile. "What can I help you understand?"

"Rumor, who you have said is very bright and energetic, had a hard time sitting still for the story," Cricket said.

"Yes," Mrs. O'Toole said.

"And to correct this, she was made to sit on a bench while the other children were running and playing?" Cricket asked.

"She needs to learn to control herself," Mrs. O'Toole said. "Losing a privilege she likes is a good lesson."

Shane suddenly thought about the point Cricket was making. The whole story actually reminded him a lot of his time in pre-school. He was pretty sure he never sat still during story time. But he didn't remember sitting on the bench for it, or his parents being called to the school.

"We'll work on reinforcing self-control at home," Cricket was saying politely. "But she will need support here at school as well. Rumor is high energy, and she definitely needs opportunities to stretch her legs and move around so she can be comfortable and focus. She was very sad when I picked her up today. But she turned it around and had an excellent afternoon after some time running and playing at the park. Fresh air and exercise are crucial for her well-being."

The truth landed on Shane like a boulder. *This* was why Rumor had been sitting quietly with a book when he got home. She must have been able to because Cricket had made sure she got all the exercise she needed to be able to relax and focus.

"What do you think?" Mrs. O'Toole asked, turning to Shane.

A rush of thoughts and emotions threatened to drown him as he thought about his own experience as a restless kid. He had been so similar to Rumor, but things had been different for him, as if the world were making everything easier on him. He'd had every opportunity to play outside, and he'd never been punished for wiggling or pacing.

"I think that my daughter shouldn't feel ashamed for being herself," he said, willing his voice not to shake. "She's high energy, just like I was. But I don't remember anyone saying I was out of control."

Boys will be boys, he remembered hearing in laughing adult voices.

"I bumped into another parent in the park," Cricket said. "His son is in Miss Cabrera's class, and he mentioned that in that classroom they set timers and have dance parties throughout the day, to help the kids get their excess energy out. Is that something Rumor's class could try? I think it might help her a lot."

"Mm," Mrs. O'Toole hummed, looking like she wanted to roll her eyes. "I think we all have lots to think about. Thank you for coming in today."

"I'm so glad we did," Cricket said, rising and offering Mrs. O'Toole her hand with a smile.

Mrs. O'Toole arose more slowly, but she shook Cricket's hand, and Shane's too when he offered it.

As they headed out of the classroom and into the hallway, Cricket's contribution today landed on him.

It wasn't just that she had stood up for Rumor in that meeting and advocated for her needs. She actually *understood* his daughter.

Emotion swirled in his chest again, heating his blood and making him feel almost light-headed.

20

NATALIE

Natalie headed out into the cold winter afternoon, relieved to drink in the fresh air as she jogged down the stairs and into the parking lot.

She wasn't particularly good at confrontations, and while things had stayed polite in there, her heart was still pounding.

In the moment though, it had been very, very easy to stand up for Rumor.

"Natalie," Shane said breathlessly, jogging up to join her by the truck.

She turned to him and was struck by the color in his cheeks.

His blue eyes were burning with emotion and his chiseled jaw was clenched.

"Are you okay?" she asked him.

"I'm more than okay," he told her, his voice deep with feeling. "You were incredible."

"I-I was?" she murmured.

"The way you stood up for her," he said. "The way you

stood up for *me*. No one has ever done something like that for us before."

He reached out, taking her hand and wrapping it in both of his.

"Thank you, Natalie," he said.

Her heart was pounding so hard she almost didn't notice that he had used her name instead of her nickname. His hands were warm and comforting, and the look of naked emotion on his face made it impossible for her to look away.

"Shane," she murmured, uncertain what was happening.

He leaned down, as if to listen, but his eyes were on her lips.

She felt breathless, unable to believe that what she had dreamed of so many times was actually happening.

Suddenly, the sound of the church bells reverberated in the air, so loud it was startling.

Shane let go of her hands and straightened. He looked like he was waking up after being hypnotized.

Shame washed over Natalie, and she turned away, scurrying to the passenger side of the truck where she could pull herself together without him seeing her.

Of course he didn't actually want to kiss her. She was still just Chris's tag-along little sister. She was a good babysitter, but that didn't mean he was going to fall in love with her. Guys like Shane ended up with popular girls like MaryLou or beautiful ones like Amanda.

But that didn't mean he wasn't a good guy, or that they couldn't continue to have a friendship. She just had to remember her place, that was all.

She took a deep breath and clambered up into the truck as the bells finished tolling, plastering a smile on her face.

Shane got in a moment later, looking a little disgruntled. She could hardly blame him. He'd almost let the emotions of the moment make him do something he didn't want to do.

"Do you think Miss O'Toole will do anything differently now with Rumor?" she asked, desperate to get some distance between the almost-maybe-kiss and the present.

"She didn't seem convinced," Shane said. "But I am."

"What do you mean?" Natalie asked.

"When I came home, Rumor was calmer than I've ever seen her in the afternoon," he said with a smile, as if the memory made him happy. "And I know it's because you took the time to make sure she ran and played and had fun today."

"She's fun to hang out with," Natalie said, thinking about watching the little girl with the chestnut curls dash around the park with the cousin. "It was no big deal."

"It's a very big deal," he told her. "I feel bad for not realizing sooner that she probably needs all the things I had at her age - a chance to be outside and get dirty, to wear herself out."

"Sometimes it seems like we have different expectations of girls than we do of boys, without even thinking about it," Natalie said carefully. "Besides, when you and I grew up, everyone spent more time outside anyway. There wasn't as much on tv."

He laughed at that, and she relaxed a little.

"Mrs. O'Toole wouldn't have been a teacher for this long if she didn't like kids," she said. "I'm sure she'll accommodate Rumor. She just might have to do it on her own terms."

"You know, you're pretty good at reading people," he said with a smile.

"Thanks," she said, feeling a funny little burst of pride. She'd never thought of reading people as a great skill. It was more of a defense mechanism. But she would take the compliment. She hadn't had all that many lately, and it felt good.

They drove on in friendly silence as the familiar scenery of Trinity Falls melted by outside.

In the absence of conversation, her mind went back to the moment outside the truck, and the way his eyes had fixed on her mouth.

He wasn't going to kiss me. He wasn't going to kiss me, she told herself as they drove.

Hopefully, by the time they got home, she would forget about it. It was good enough to have a job and people she liked in her life. There was no need to go looking for romance where there wasn't any.

21

SHANE

Later that evening, Shane finished hitching the horses up to the carriage and gave each an encouraging pat.

The two were huffing excitedly, their breath pluming in the cold.

Everyone on the farm loved the holiday season, even if they had to work a little harder. The horses, the hands, even the college kids who worked bagging and checking folks out in the shop got excited when they traded their regular aprons for red and green every year.

Shane normally felt like the Scrooge of the bunch, secretly resenting the workload that took him from his kids, and even more secretly licking his wounds over losing Lou during what was supposed to be the happiest time of the year.

But today, he felt centered somehow, as if he were finally anchored in place in the present.

Cricket's help today meant a lot. It felt like having a partner again.

That's why I almost kissed her, he told himself. *I was just caught up in the moment, feeling like she cared.*

He tried not to let himself picture the startled look on her sweet face when the bells rang, and he got himself together enough to actually look at her eyes instead of that pretty mouth.

He'd been so busy following his own feelings that he hadn't stopped to think about how she felt, or what she wanted.

He was lucky she let him change the subject instead of just quitting on the spot. The last thing a promising young woman like Natalie Bell needed was to tether herself to a grumpy old widower like him.

But...

But in the moment, the way she breathed his name, it had really felt like she wanted him to kiss her.

Even if she did, he wasn't ready to lose his best friend over it.

Chris called less and less the longer he was away. And when he did respond to Shane's calls and emails, his tone was off. Chris was obviously having some kind of issue, and Shane had no idea what it was.

How could Shane move in on Chris's little sister while he was serving his country and obviously going through something? The idea of it was unforgivable.

I need to get out of the house. Maybe I should just let Sadie Wilkinson set me up with someone, like she's been begging to do.

He had no interest in marrying again after Lou. And dating just to scratch an itch was an idea that held no allure for him.

But maybe if he had a woman in his life, someone more appropriate for him than Cricket, it would help him stop thinking about her.

He had almost reached the house when he saw they

were all outside waiting for him.

"Daddy," Rumor yelled, waving her arms, like he might think someone else on the farm was calling to him.

"Hey, Sugar," he yelled back. "You ready for a carriage ride?"

She nodded, and Cricket took her hand on the steps.

He was happy to see that Rumor was bundled up, since it was likely to get dark while they were out. And he was delighted to see Wyatt was there, too. Last year, he'd had to practically pry the kid out of his room.

This year, he was chatting non-stop to Cricket. Shane wished he knew what they were talking about that had Wyatt so involved.

"This is so exciting," Cricket said to Shane as they joined him on the front lawn.

"Are you ready?" he asked her.

"Very ready," she said. "Are there any rules we should know about?"

"Just have fun," he said. "And keep your hands inside the carriage."

"And don't scare Peanut Butter and Pickles," Rumor said.

"Those are the horses," Cricket said, nodding.

Rumor began telling her the names of all the other horses on the farm.

Shane reached out and tousled Wyatt's hair.

"How's it going?" he asked the boy.

"Fine," Wyatt said, shrugging.

"I'm glad you're coming," Shane told him.

"I always come on the first carriage ride, Dad," Wyatt said, his shy smile lighting up his face.

"I know," Shane told him. "I'm glad you're not too cool for it, now that you're a teenager. I never was either."

Wyatt frowned.

"What?" Shane asked.

"Nothing," Wyatt said, shoving his hands in his pockets.

For a minute he looked so much older and more serious than he ever had before, and Shane's heart gave a helpless twinge.

What was he supposed to do when he could see his son disappearing into himself but there were no other signs of trouble?

Wyatt's grades were fine, and his behavior reports at school were stellar. He did his chores, and he even kept his room neat. And Shane didn't see any signs the boy was being bullied.

He'd even taken him in to see Dr. Wilkinson for a private check-up, and instructed the kindly doctor to see if he could get the boy to open up.

But Dr. Wilkinson had simply said Wyatt seemed reserved but content, and that it was normal for kids to reflect more and talk less at his age.

Shane just couldn't shake the feeling that something more was wrong. And he ached to fix it.

"Hi, Peanut Butter. Hi, Pickles," Rumor said in a calm but excited voice when they reached the barn.

The two horses were waiting out front with the carriage behind them, looking very shiny after his hard work today. Rumor walked right up to the giant creatures, reaching up to stroke their velvety noses.

The horses whickered at her, snuffling her little hands for treats.

"Here, Rumor," Cricket said, pulling a carrot out of her jacket. "Want one, Wyatt?"

He took it with a smile.

Shane and Cricket stepped back at the same time to watch the kids feed the horses.

"This is amazing," she murmured.

"Do you like horses?" he asked.

"I love them, in theory," she said. "I've never really spent time with them."

"If you ever want to learn to ride, I'd be glad to teach you," he heard himself offer, and then immediately felt like an idiot. If she wanted to learn to ride a horse, she would have had plenty of opportunities growing up in Trinity Falls.

"Seriously?" she asked, looking like he had offered her the winning lotto numbers. "I would love that. Maybe when your busy season is over?"

"I'm sure we can find a time before that," he told her.

"Let's go," Rumor squeaked excitedly.

"Okay, kiddo," Shane told her fondly. "Hop in."

"I'll be in the middle," Rumor announced, scooting to the center of the front seat.

"Well, you know where I'm gonna be," Shane told her.

Wyatt started to climb in.

"No," Rumor yelled. "I want to be between Daddy and Cricket."

"Rumor," Cricket began.

"It's fine," Wyatt said. "I'll be on the end next to you."

"Awesome," Cricket said, helping Rumor up and then climbing in next to her, followed by Wyatt.

Shane walked over to the other side to grab the big blankets from the back and hand them out.

"Okay, gang," he said. "Bundle up."

"Like this, Cricket," Rumor said, pulling the blanket over their laps.

"Oh, yes, that's going to be nice and cozy," Cricket said. "Even though it's cold outside, we'll be snug as a bug in a rug."

Rumor let out a howl of laugher.

Shane smiled and climbed in, letting Rumor cover his lap with one of the blankets and pulling part of it over her little legs too.

"Like this," Rumor said happily, patting his leg. "Snug as a rug bug."

He smiled at the way she tried to echo Cricket's words.

"Are we ready, guys?" he asked.

"Yes," Wyatt said.

"Yes, yes, yes," Rumor chirped, wiggling a little beside him.

He glanced over at Cricket.

"Yes, absolutely," she said.

"Okay, remember this isn't like driving a car," he teased her. "There are bumps."

"I'll hold on tight," she laughed.

He clucked to the horses, and they pulled forward, which set the bells jingling.

"Oh my gosh, the bells," Cricket said, laughing with delight. "This is amazing. I feel like I'm in a Christmas movie."

He smiled, soaking in her happiness.

Normally, he just took the kids on a jaunt around the barn and shops and then past Grandma's, so she could take photos from the porch.

But he found himself wanting to give Cricket the whole experience.

"Who wants to explore the Christmas tree forest?" he asked.

"Me, me, me," Rumor squealed.

"Awesome," Wyatt said.

Shane glanced over at his son, pleased to see him enjoying himself doing something that had nothing to do with screens.

"That would be amazing," Cricket said.

Shane clucked to the horses again and they broke into a gentle trot. It was no faster than they ran with the guests every weekend during the holiday season, but everyone onboard started giggling anyway.

He joined them, drinking in the cold, sweet air.

The thought that it smelled like snow had barely occurred to him when the first soft white flakes began to drift down.

"It's snowing," Rumor yelled.

"Snow day, snow day," Wyatt chanted softly.

Rumor chanted with him while Cricket let her head fall backward to laugh.

"Do you guys taste the snowflakes?" she asked them a moment later.

"Cricket, you're too old," Rumor whispered, scandalized.

Shane barely repressed a laugh and glanced over at Cricket, hoping she wouldn't be offended.

"You're right. Usually I'm far too dignified," Cricket agreed, winking at Shane. "But these big lacy ones are irresistible."

He watched, transfixed, as she opened her mouth and caught a snowflake on her tongue.

"Now me, now me," Rumor yelled.

"You have to stick out your tongue," Cricket reminded her.

He smiled when Wyatt joined, the three of them laughing and eating snowflakes as fast as they fell.

Rumor's chestnut curls were dotted with white lace, and Cricket's long dark hair was decorated with the icy crystals, too.

Wyatt wore a battered cowboy hat, one of Shane's old ones. It protected his dark hair from the snow, and made

Shane realize how much his son was starting to look like a small mirror.

"What, Dad?" Wyatt asked, his eyes still laughing.

"Nothing," Shane said. "You look good in that hat is all."

"I look good in all hats," Wyatt decided.

"He's not wrong," Cricket said, nodding sagely. "He's definitely a hat man."

"Hat man, hat man, hat man," Rumor repeated, then laughed her head off.

The horses hung a right into the rows of Christmas trees without any guidance. They had done the run so many times, it was second nature to them. Shane let himself relax and enjoy the scent of pine needles, the sounds of happiness, and the warmth of his daughter, shaking with laughter as she snuggled up to him.

Cricket looked over at him with a grateful smile.

"Thank you," she said softly.

"For what?" he asked. "This is just a little fun at the end of the day."

"Nana and I always wanted to do a carriage ride," she said with a wry smile. "We never did get around to it."

"Here at the farm?" he asked.

She nodded with a smile, emotion shining in her eyes.

"I would have taken the two of you out anytime," he told her sincerely. "I'm only sorry you never asked."

"She would be so happy that I'm here now," Cricket said softly. "It's so much better than we ever imagined. It's... magical."

Shane nodded, too moved to speak.

But he was thinking that if there was magic here, Cricket had brought a whole lot of it herself, breathing new life into their old tradition just by coming along.

"We have to sing Christmas carols," Rumor yelled.

"Is that part of the tradition?" Cricket asked her.

"No, but it's *fun*," Rumor said.

"Let's do *Jingle Bell Rock*," Cricket suggested.

They started singing and even Shane joined in after a moment. Cricket had a clear, pleasant voice, and Rumor's enthusiasm was infectious.

Only Wyatt wasn't singing.

"Come on, Wyatt," Cricket encouraged him.

He shook his head and looked down, embarrassed.

"Wyatt only likes angry music," Rumor told her.

"What?" Cricket asked.

"It's metal," Wyatt said. "It's not angry."

"Oh, I get it," Cricket said. "Well, we can just sing the metal version of *Jingle Bell Rock*."

"Cricket, what are you *talking* about?" Rumor laughed.

To Shane's intense surprise, Cricket fluffed up her hair until it was a tangly looking mess. Then she began to toss her head back and forth exaggeratedly, sending her wild locks into a cascade.

Wyatt cracked a smile and Rumor began to giggle.

Cricket started yelling out the lyrics with a pretty good imitation of a sore throat inducing heavy metal rasp. By the time she got to the second line, Wyatt was singing, too. And he actually sounded awesome.

Rumor joined them as Cricket began to play the air guitar.

Shane smiled and shook his head at the sight of them - all three losing themselves in the silliness of their over-the-top rendition of the classic song.

"Come on, Dad," Wyatt yelled.

The next thing he knew, he was rocking out as the snow fell, soft and beautiful around them all.

22

NATALIE

Natalie looked around the table at all the smiling, happy faces.

Mrs. Cassidy had prepared a huge meal of roasted chicken with herbed stuffing, root vegetables, salad, and rolls with honeyed butter. The larger platters were interspersed with dishes of raw veggies and nuts.

The kids had eaten more than she thought they could fit in their bellies, and she was feeling almost as stuffed as the chicken herself.

The food was almost as good as the company. Mr. Cassidy had been telling funny stories about Shane and his siblings all night.

"Coffee's brewing," Mrs. Cassidy said, winking at Natalie. "I only wish I had time to make some dessert."

Wyatt looked up from his plate and right into Natalie's eyes. his expression questioning and a bit nervous.

"No worries there," Natalie said. "Wyatt whipped up some banana bread after school today. We brought it with us, just in case. Want to grab it from the kitchen, Wyatt?"

Wyatt slid out of his seat, looking like what he really wanted was to be invisible.

The sight of it tugged at her heart. Of all places, Wyatt should feel confident here at his grandparents' house, where he was so clearly beloved by everyone.

"I'll get the coffee things," Shane offered, hopping up to join his son in the kitchen.

"I didn't know Wyatt was interested in cooking," Mrs. Cassidy confided in Natalie. "At least, not until you gave me a heads up about dessert."

"He's a wonderful cook," Natalie said as Wyatt came back in. "So knowledgeable and inventive."

Wyatt tried and failed to hide his smile.

"Lovely," Mrs. Cassidy said, looking down at the neatly wrapped loaf of banana bread. "What's that on top?"

"A pecan crust," Wyatt told her excitedly. "I saw it on the *BBKC,* and then modified it slightly because of a video I saw on BeeBop."

"You watch the *Big British Kitchen Competition*?" Mrs. Cassidy asked, her eyes lighting up.

"Yeah," he said. "I love it."

His grandmother shook her head in wonder as she sliced the bread on a wooden cutting board.

"Oh, it looks nice and moist," she said.

"But it should be cooked all the way through," he told her, leaning intently over the table to look.

"Perfectly cooked all the way through," Mrs. Cassidy said. "And..."

"*No soggy bottom,*" they both sang out together.

Shane met Natalie's eyes across the table and smiled warmly. She had no idea what Wyatt and Mrs. Cassidy were talking about, and she was pretty sure Shane didn't either. But it was nice to see them bonding over the bread.

The whole evening had been so nice. It felt like the old days, when Chris was home and the two of them and Nana always had people over for supper. She missed the lovely smells, the hustle-bustle, and the quiet talk at the table when everyone had eaten.

And she missed her brother. He'd been in touch less than usual lately, and it was starting to worry her.

"Now what was that other thing you said you were watching, Wyatt?" his grandmother asked. "Bee sting?"

"BeeBop?" Wyatt asked, laughing.

"Yes," she replied. "What is that?"

"It's a social media app for your phone, Grandma," he told her. "But instead of pictures, you post little videos, and you can add music too, if you want. There are tons of baking tips on there."

"How wonderful," she replied. "Can you put it on my phone so I can look at it too?"

"Of course," he said excitedly. "Where's your phone?"

"It's plugged in on the kitchen table," she told him, and he jogged off to retrieve it.

"What can I do?" Rumor asked plaintively.

"Oh, your grandfather was hoping you could gather up the plates, since that's usually his job," Mrs. Cassidy said. "But I think you might be too little for that."

"I'm not too little," Rumor protested.

"Okay, then just carry one or two at a time," her grandmother said. "You can put them by the sink for me, okay?"

Rumor hopped off her chair and got right to work, carrying a plate and silverware into the kitchen.

"Mom, she really is little," Shane said quietly.

"Don't be silly. She's not too little to help," his mother said. "Besides, this is just our everyday china, the good stuff is in the buffet."

"Okay, Grandma," Wyatt said, heading back into the room with her phone in his hand. "I started you an account and your recommended feed is populating now based on your interests and location."

"Incredible," Mrs. Cassidy said. "I hear that young people today have a real passion for sourdough. Hopefully, I can learn something."

"Oh," Wyatt said, looking down at the screen. "Oh wow."

"What is it?" Mrs. Cassidy asked.

"Natalie," Wyatt said. "You're buzzing."

"Oh, I'm barely ever on BeeBop, and I've never posted anything," Natalie said, laughing. "I can't be buzzing on there."

As Wyatt walked over, she could hear surf guitar music playing from the phone.

He held it out and she took it from him, wondering what in the world she was about to see.

The scene in the video was familiar. It was the interior of Jolly Beans, and a boy was holding up posters asking a girl to the Snow Ball.

"We were here during this," she said, looking up at Shane, whose eyes were fixed on the video. A line was forming on his brow.

She looked back at the video and saw herself standing by the counter and then moving forward.

No...

But the kid taking the video had seen what was going to happen and the camera focused in, capturing the moment when she slammed into Holly.

The video slowed to give a frame-by-frame rendition of one of the most mortifying moments of her life while a voice in the soundtrack kicked in.

Ha-ha-ha-ha... wipe out.

She shot out of her chair, abandoning the phone on the tabletop as she ran for the front door. She had no plan for what would happen when she got outside. She only knew she needed to get away.

The front door opened easily, letting in a blast of snowy air. She stepped outside and closed it behind her as hot tears prickled in her eyes.

The cold wind felt good against her burning cheeks. She walked to the curve of the porch so that no one could see her from the front windows and then she let herself sob.

Shame bubbled up in her chest and she cried hard, not like a movie heroine, with tears sliding silently down her cheeks, but in a storm of sobs and tears and gasps.

It had been a hard year, not just losing Nana without Chris around, but before that, too. Things in the city hadn't been going well, and she was coming to terms with the fact that her non-existent music career was basically never going to take off.

And every year closer to thirty made it feel like she might never have the family she had dreamed of either.

Moving back to Trinity Falls to be with Nana had made her see the sweet little town with different eyes, and feel like maybe this was her place in the world after all.

And her time with Rumor, Wyatt and Shane made her feel like even if she didn't have her own family, maybe there was a place for her with them, as their nanny.

But the video reminded her of everything she had let herself forget. Trinity Falls was a tiny town with a long memory. No one would forget this video, just like no one would forget the dreamy girl with the guitar who went off to make a fool of herself in New York.

The holiday season would wrap up, and Shane would

wish her well, and she would be unable to find any other work here.

It had been one thing to be miserable in New York when it was what she thought she wanted. But having to go back there because she couldn't even find a waitressing job here made her feel worse than a failure.

She longed for her Nana and her big brother more than she ever had - more than when she had stood alone at the funeral accepting condolences, more than the nights she had spent alone since then, trying to sort through Nana's possessions.

She heard the front door click and heavy footsteps heading her way.

She tried wiping away her tears and snot, but it was no use. She was a cold, wet, sniffling, pathetic mess.

"Oh, Natalie," Shane said simply, pulling her into his arms.

And somehow, even though she'd already been crying hard, that simple kindness really opened the floodgates.

She let her head rest against his muscular chest and cried like her heart was broken.

"It's just social media," he murmured. "That stuff blows over quickly, I'm told."

"It's not that," she sobbed. "I mean it is that, but it's everything. I feel like I don't matter."

"What are you talking about?" he asked, pulling back slightly.

"There's no meaning in my life," she murmured stupidly. "I'm not anything to anyone."

"Were you even here tonight?" he demanded, wrapping his big hands around her shoulders, his cerulean eyes flashing with passion and fixed on hers. "You helped my son connect with his grandmother. You defended Rumor at school, and helped her get the time she needed outside. You mean everything to us."

His hands tightened and his jaw clenched.

Suddenly, her pain was forgotten, and she was mesmerized with the raw emotion on his face.

"I'm sorry, Natalie," Wyatt said from the doorway, breaking the spell. "I didn't realize what that was, and I didn't mean to hurt your feelings by making you watch it."

"Oh, Wyatt," she said, feeling awful that he was seeing her tearstained face. "It's not your fault. I'm *so* glad you showed me, so I didn't have to find out from someone else, or out in town or something."

"Everyone gets made fun of sometimes," Wyatt said. "The kids at school call me *Quiet Wyatt*."

She could sense Shane's surprise and discomfort.

"That's ridiculous," she said. "They clearly haven't heard you sing Christmas carols."

Wyatt laughed and she wrapped an arm around his shoulder.

"Listen, I don't want to terrify your little sister going back in there like this," she said. "Do you have a tissue or anything?"

"I'll get you one," he said. "Wait right here."

She turned back to Shane as Wyatt disappeared into the house again.

"He never told me that," Shane said softly. "I had no idea the kids made fun of him."

"Like he said, it's normal," she said gently. "Kids are trying out new things at his age, including being mean. Most of them will decide it's a bad fit."

Shane just shook his head.

Wyatt came out with a wad of tissues, and Natalie cleaned herself up as best she could.

"You're a lifesaver, Wyatt," she told him. "And I'm going to be totally cheered up when I eat some of your banana bread, I promise."

They headed back in, Shane trailing behind them.

She glanced back to make sure he was okay.

He had a thoughtful look on his face that told her exactly nothing.

23

NATALIE

When they got back inside, Natalie was grateful to see that Rumor and her grandfather were curled up on the family room sofa, reading together, and Mrs. Cassidy was working in the open kitchen. Everyone was completely in their own world, not waiting to see how she was doing.

Wyatt drifted into the kitchen, and she followed, automatically gathering up the dishes by the sink and scraping them into the trash while Mrs. Cassidy wrapped up leftovers.

"You don't have to do that, sweetheart," Mrs. Cassidy said. "You've had a busy day already. Why don't you go put your feet up? We'll have our dessert and coffee when I get finished with the dinner things."

"I like helping," Natalie said. "Besides, you can't cook for six people and then clean up by yourself."

"She won't let me help her," Mr. Cassidy piped up from the family room.

"You're supposed to be healing up," she retorted. "Now

read your book, my granddaughter wants to know how it ends."

"Stuff and nonsense," Mr. Cassidy muttered, waggling his eyebrows, which made Rumor laugh.

"I'm going to check on the horses," Shane said.

"I'll help," Wyatt told him.

They headed out, leaving Natalie alone with Mrs. Cassidy.

Natalie finished with the plates and moved on to washing the dishes. Though there was a dishwasher, she couldn't help noticing the drain board on the counter, so she got to work hand-washing.

"Girl after my own heart," Mrs. Cassidy said. "I never could stand that thing."

"The dishwasher?" Natalie asked.

"Seems like it wastes a lot of water for just two people," Mrs. Cassidy said sadly. "For a night like tonight, I guess it's worth using, but I always think hand washing gets them cleaner."

"Agreed," Natalie told her.

"If you want to keep washing, I'll dry and put away," Mrs. Cassidy suggested.

"Perfect," Natalie said. "I don't know where anything goes."

They worked in friendly silence for a few minutes.

"Shane mentioned you've been doing some cooking and shopping," Mrs. Cassidy said eventually. "That's very kind of you."

"I have nothing else to do while Rumor is at school," Natalie said, shrugging. "If you want, I don't mind shopping for you, while Mr. Cassidy is laid up. Just make me a list."

"Oh honey, you're tempting my good morals," Mrs. Cassidy laughed.

"I really don't mind," Natalie laughed. "I'm going there and coming back to the farm anyway. My good morals tell me we shouldn't have two cars making that journey when we could have one."

"I just might take you up on that," Mrs. Cassidy said. "At least for the next few weeks, it would be a real help. Joe can't walk around the store, and he can't be trusted here."

"What do you mean?" Natalie asked, scandalized.

"Oh, he thinks he can sneak off and do his chores," Mrs. Cassidy said, throwing her hands up in the air. "And I tried dropping him off at Jolly Beans the other day while I shopped, but he didn't care for it."

"The music is too loud," Mr. Cassidy complained from the other room.

"Yes, Joe, I know," Mrs. Cassidy said, shaking her head and smiling. "And the coffee was too expensive."

"Not just expensive," he said. "It's too complicated, and it doesn't taste right."

"He tried the library once, too," Mrs. Cassidy confided. "But they said he was too noisy."

"Minerva Wallace kept trying to shush me," Mr. Cassidy laughed, thumping his thigh. "She's nothing but a volunteer, and I told her so."

"Joseph Aaron Cassidy," Mrs. Cassidy scolded. "People go to the library to study or read quietly. They don't come there to hear you and Reggie Webb shooting the shinola about the almanac and gossiping about the man that bought Lavington Farm like a couple of hens."

"Sounds like we need another café," Natalie laughed. "Something louder than the library and quieter than Jolly Beans."

"The *last* thing this town needs is another trendy coffee shop," Mr. Cassidy said, with great finality.

They finished up cleaning the kitchen and had just set out plates and cups for coffee and dessert when Shane came back with snow in his hair, Wyatt trailing behind him.

Their cheeks were pink, and their eyes were sparkling. To Natalie, they looked like the perfect picture of farm men.

"Ready for dessert, boys?" Mrs. Cassidy asked.

This time, when they all gathered round, Natalie wasn't fretting about the buzzing video anymore. She was firmly entrenched in the moment.

And as exquisitely delicious as the dessert was, no coffee could ever taste richer or banana bread sweeter than the goodness of sharing time with the Cassidy family.

24

SHANE

Just before dawn, Shane raked fresh straw into the stalls, working on autopilot as his mind played and replayed last night's events.

Every time he closed his eyes he saw Natalie, talking with Rumor, cooking and singing with Wyatt, laughing in the kitchen with his mom, and crying her eyes out while he held her close.

There were a million reasons why he shouldn't tell her about his feelings.

She worked for him, she was his best friend's little sister, she was at a vulnerable place in her life...

He had spent the past few days trying to convince himself to wait. If he could just make it until she was out of his house and had another job, if he could wait until Chris was home so he could talk with him, if he could wait until the pain she felt over losing her Nana was a part of her, and not so new, then pursuing her might not feel so wrong.

But after yesterday, he knew that waiting wasn't an option.

His feelings for her filled him to overflowing. He had

awoken this morning afraid he wouldn't make it to the breakfast table without declaring his intentions.

Breathe, he reminded himself.

Raking out the sweet straw in the next stall, he reminded himself that he was going to take care of at least one of his reasons not to act today. He had emailed her brother and asked him to call.

Though Chris had been strangely quiet this past year, their friendship was strong enough that Shane was sure he would get in touch as soon as he could.

As if the thought had summoned the call, his phone began to chime.

He snatched it from his pocket and swiped to answer before the second ring.

"Shane," he said.

"Hey."

Chris's voice was a little tinny, but Shane would have known it anywhere.

"Thanks for calling back," Shane said. "How are you?"

"I'm alright," Chris said. "You?"

"Better, now that your little sister is taking care of my kids," Shane said, jumping right in.

There was a pause.

"She's what?" Chris asked.

"I bumped into her at the café," Shane told him. "And she was looking for work. I've been so tied up at the farm. I told her I could use help with the kids."

Another pause. Shane figured they must not have a great connection.

"Hey, that's great," Chris said. "Thanks, man. You've always looked out for her, and I appreciate it, especially since I'm not there."

Shane felt a pang of guilt.

"She's doing a great job," he said. "It's really no favor. She's helping me a lot."

If that wasn't the understatement of the year, he didn't know what was.

"Keep her out of trouble, will you?" Chris asked quietly. "I know she's feeling down about the music stuff, and even more so about Nana. It would be too easy for some idiot to take advantage of her right now."

Shane opened his mouth and closed it again, unable to think of a single word to say to get this conversation back on track.

I am that idiot.

"You still there?" Chris asked.

"Yeah, man, I'm still here," Shane said. "Natalie is a really wonderful person, everyone knows that. And I know this has been a hard year for you both—"

"Listen," Chris said, before Shane could launch himself into a segue. "About that, I have some news, but you need to keep it a secret from her."

"Okay," Shane said.

What was one more secret, when he was already holding back so much?

"I'm coming home," Chris said. "I'll be there next weekend."

"No way," Shane exclaimed. "She'll be so happy. So, you'll be home for Christmas?"

"Sure will," Chris said, a smile in his voice. "Though I don't know what I'll do when I'm there. Is anyone out that way hiring? I don't want to sit on my butt."

"Are you kidding?" Shane asked. "Some guy from the city bought Livingston Farm. He's hiring anyone with a pulse. No one around here can find hands. I'm desperate myself."

"You're not desperate anymore," Chris said. "If you need help, I'll be there."

"Don't offer so fast," Shane said, his better angels guiding him. "You might get twice the pay from the Livingston guy."

"You're my best friend, idiot," Chris laughed. "I've always got your back."

"Thank you," Shane said, guilt weighing heavy on his heart.

"Look, I've got to go," Chris said. "Don't breathe a word to her."

"Scout's honor," Shane told him.

He signed off the call in a haze of worry, his stomach feeling like it was filled with lead.

I'll wait until he's here, he told himself at last, sliding the phone back into his pocket. *I'll wait until he can see for himself how much she belongs in this family, and how fiercely I would treasure her...*

25

NATALIE

In her dream, Natalie spun around the high school gym in Shane's strong arms while Christmas music played.

Giant snowflake decorations hung from the ceiling, and when she looked around, she realized they were surrounded by teenagers.

She glanced down at herself to see the pretty sea foam green dress she had worn to the Snow Ball when she was in eighth grade and Brad Williams had asked her.

But she wasn't with Brad Williams now, she was with Shane, the one she had wanted to be with even then.

He gazed down at her, his piercing blue eyes filled with emotion.

She felt like she was melting.

Suddenly, the music stopped.

The crowd around them parted to reveal a photo projected onto the wall behind them.

It was the picture of Shane with Lou, his head tilted up in laughter as Lou gazed happily into the camera, her dark eyes shining, chestnut curls cascading down her back.

A sense of having betrayed her lanced Natalie's heart.

No, no, no...

She woke herself up still trying to say the word.

Blinking, she took in the room, which was suffused with sunlight.

She almost panicked before remembering that it was Saturday. The kids didn't have school, so she was technically off-duty.

Taking a deep breath, she sat up and forced herself to remember that it was only a dream.

Besides, she couldn't betray Lou with Shane, when nothing was going on between them in the first place.

But you want there to be something...

She leapt out of bed and freshened up in the bathroom, trying to convince herself there was nothing wrong with dreaming about dancing with Shane.

But it was hard not to acknowledge what her subconscious was obviously trying to tell her. Even in a fantasy, being here meant grappling with memories of Lou - his, the kids', even her own limited memories of the older girl back in high school.

Living here, and caring about Lou's family, dipping a toe into what her role had been - all of it was meaningful, whether she let herself keep crushing on Shane or managed to nip it in the bud.

I'm so sorry, Lou, she thought. *I love your family, but I know everything would be better for them if you were still here.*

But she still had an uneasy feeling. She padded downstairs in her makeshift pajamas without showering and dressing first like she normally did in the mornings. She still hadn't made it back to the house to grab her forgotten PJs, so she was wearing one of Shane's old baseball t-shirts and a pair of yoga pants.

You just want to sleep in his shirts, a little voice said in the back of her head.

She shook it off and headed downstairs, figuring she could at least make breakfast for the kids before she decided what to do with her day. Shane had probably gone off to work with the horses hours ago.

"Cricket?" Rumor said sleepily as she passed her room.

"Hey, love," Natalie said. "I'm going to make some pancakes, okay? Want me to wake you up when they're ready?"

Rumor made a happy *mm* noise as she wiggled out of bed, and Natalie smiled to herself and moved down the hallway toward the stairs just as Wyatt came out of the bathroom.

"Morning, Wyatt," she said.

"Morning," he replied with a smile.

"I was going to make breakfast, if you feel like helping," she told him.

"Sure," he said.

She headed down the stairs to get started but paused as soon as she hit the bottom step.

It smelled like fresh coffee was brewing.

Figuring Shane might have set the coffeemaker on a timer for her, she headed for the kitchen and froze when she got to the threshold.

A woman with chestnut curls like Rumor's cascading down her back stood at the sink, looking out the window at the snow-covered farm.

Lou.

Natalie thought her heart would stop beating.

"Aunt Jenna," Rumor yelled, her little footsteps pounding the floorboards as she ran for the kitchen.

"Hey, Aunt Jenna," Wyatt said as he joined his sister in the kitchen.

"Hey kids," Jenna said, turning to wrap them up in her arms. "And you must be little Cricket Bell, all grown up. What's wrong? You look like you've seen a ghost."

That was so close to the truth of what she thought she had seen that Natalie tried to swallow and speak at the same time and ended up spluttering a little before she was able to reply to Lou's twin sister.

"Uh, hi," she said, finally recovering. "It's great to see you."

Jenna eyed her up and down, then gave her a warm smile.

"Shane said you've been working hard all week," she said. "I thought I'd spend the weekend so you can be sure to actually take your time off. I try to swing by once a week or so to see my niece and nephew."

"That's wonderful," Natalie said, meaning it. "Do you still live in town?"

"Philly," Jenna said, shaking her head. "It's no New York, but it's just far away enough to have access to an art scene. And just close enough to be able to swing by and chew the fat with these rug rats whenever I feel like it."

She rustled Wyatt's shock of dark hair and he grinned at her.

"That's really cool," Natalie said. "Are you an artist now?"

"I've got a day job, but yeah," Jenna said. "How about you? Are you still playing?"

It was the first time anyone in Trinity Falls had asked her about music since she'd gotten home.

It felt oddly good to be asked. Jenna didn't have the

smug look on her face of someone hoping to hear she'd failed. She seemed genuinely interested.

"Not this week," Natalie laughed. "I've been too busy, but yeah, I think I'll always play, even if it's just for myself."

"For sure," Jenna said, nodding in understanding. "It's part of you."

"You play music?" Wyatt asked.

"Oh sure," Jenna said, before Natalie could reply. "Cricket was the pride of the Trinity Falls High music program. She's unbelievable on the guitar. She even writes her own songs."

"No way," Wyatt said, his eyes widening.

Natalie smiled, feeling a little embarrassed but a lot more grateful to Jenna.

"Acoustic, not electric," she said, shrugging. "But yeah, I love music."

"You have a guitar in your room," Rumor said suddenly.

"How do you know about that?" Natalie teased. "Were you looking in my room?"

"Yes," Rumor said, nodding hard enough that her curls bounced. "I like your room."

"Me too," Natalie told her, patting her head.

"So, who wants pancakes?" Jenna asked, echoing Natalie's plan for the morning.

Everyone obviously wanted pancakes. Natalie helped Jenna plate them, while Rumor and Wyatt set the table.

"I texted Shane," Jenna said. "He should be here in time to eat with us."

She said it in such an oddly intimate way, that Natalie was afraid for a moment that Jenna knew about the feelings she was trying so desperately to hide.

Suddenly, it hit her that she was wearing his shirt. No wonder Jenna had looked her up and down a minute ago.

Blood rushed to her cheeks as she tried to find a way to answer the question no one had asked.

But there was no way to deny a relationship with Shane when Jenna hadn't accused her of anything.

"That's good," she managed. "He'll probably be hungry after working all morning."

"He always is," Jenna said, grabbing coffee mugs from the cabinet. "So, you can't be planning on staying around here all day on your day off. What are you up to?"

"I have a hot date with my Nana's house," Natalie laughed. "I've got to keep working on emptying it out to sell it. And I've got to grab my pajamas, I can't keep borrowing Shane's old shirts to sleep in."

She hoped the forced explanation sounded more natural than it felt.

"Any other hot dates planned?" Jenna asked. "I'll be spending the night, so no one needs to worry about coverage."

What in the world was that supposed to mean? Was she trying to say she would watch the kids so Natalie could go out with Shane?

She wished desperately that there was a hole she could fall into and never be seen again.

"No, no hot dates for me," Natalie laughed awkwardly.

"Ah," Jenna said, nodding thoughtfully. "Well, Trinity Falls is a tough place to be single. That's why I took this smoke-show on the road."

She indicated herself in such a silly way that Natalie couldn't hold in a smile.

"Is Philadelphia a good place for dating?" Natalie asked politely.

"I don't know, kids," Jenna said, turning to the table.

"What do you think? Have I had good luck going on dates in Philly?"

"No," they yelled back. Rumor started howling with laughter.

"My goodness," Natalie said. "It's not very nice to laugh at your aunt."

"Oh, they're completely correct," Jenna laughed. "My love life is kind of like a stand-up comedy show. Right?"

But they just kept on laughing.

"Right," Jenna said, shaking her head with a wry grin. "Comedy is about all it's good for."

"But it's *really* good comedy," Wyatt said. "Tell us about the latest one."

"Oh, you don't want to hear it," Jenna teased, sitting down at the table.

"Yes we do," Rumor squeaked.

Natalie slid into her seat to listen.

"Your dad will be here in two shakes," Jenna said, glancing at her phone. "Should I tell you about the last one while we wait for him?"

"Yes," Rumor yelled.

"Okay, but you have to promise not to touch your breakfast until he gets here, okay?" Jenna asked.

They all agreed, and Natalie found herself leaning forward to hear what Jenna was going to say.

"Do you guys know what an escape room is?" Jenna asked.

Natalie repressed a groan.

"No," Rumor said.

"Well, it's a sort of activity," Jenna told her. "You go to a building and once you get inside someone welcomes you and explains the story."

"What story?" Rumor asked.

"Each escape room has a story that goes with it," Jenna said. "The host brings you to a room with an actor in it and clues, then they lock you in the room, and you have to use the clues to solve the mystery of where to find the key. If you find the key in a certain amount of time you can get out. If you don't find the key in time the murderer gets you. That's the actor in the room, and it's obviously not real."

"That seems fun," Wyatt said. "Was it?"

"Oh, I have no idea," Jenna said, shrugging.

"You didn't go?" Wyatt asked.

"We went," Jenna said. "We got to hear about the mystery and then they locked us in the room. It was a creepy library with candles and a man who was supposed to be the murderer asleep in a chair in the corner."

"Whoa," Wyatt said.

"Scary," Rumor whispered.

"Well, only for a minute or two," Jenna said. "We went in, and my date walked right up to the actor playing the murderer and punched him in the face. Then he slammed into the locked door so hard he broke through it. And when he got into the hallway he high-fived *himself* for solving the locked room so fast."

Wyatt snorted and even Natalie couldn't hold in a horrified gasp of laughter.

"Not really though, right?" Wyatt asked.

"My hand to God," Jenna said solemnly, lifting her hand. "I couldn't make that up if I tried."

"You're not allowed to hit people," Rumor said sternly.

"You most certainly are not," Jenna agreed. "And that's why the police came right away, and my date was taken to the local jail. And as they led him away, he tried to demand his money back."

At that, even Natalie laughed her head off, and Rumor

joined her after a minute.

"What's going on in here?" Shane's voice boomed through the hallway. "There's only one person who makes you laugh like that."

"Aunt Jenna is here," Rumor yelled, shooting out of her seat and taking off down the hall to greet him.

A moment later, Shane appeared in the doorway, with Rumor on his hip, her chubby arms wrapped around his neck.

"Nice to see you, sis," he said fondly to Jenna.

Natalie smiled at the idea that his sister-in-law would always be his sister in his eyes.

"Aunt Jenna was locked in a room and her date punched somebody in the face," Rumor told him.

"Is there someone I need to teach a lesson to?" he asked Jenna.

"It was a locked room mystery," Jenna said. "And no, the local police have probably talked some sense into him by now."

"Can't you come home and date a nice farmer, like everyone else?" Shane asked. "I've got friends I could introduce you to, nice guys."

"I'm not settling down with a farmer," Jenna said, rolling her eyes. "I'll take my chances in a locked room."

"Suit yourself," Shane said with a smile, placing Rumor down and pulling out the chair next to Natalie's.

She looked up at him and he winked at her as he sat down.

A shiver of awareness went down her spine.

Determined not to react, she shoveled pancakes into her mouth to drown it out.

He's only being nice, she reminded herself.

26

SHANE

Shane pushed back from the breakfast table, feeling content.

It wasn't just a full belly making him feel at ease. It was having everyone together at the table, laughing and enjoying the meal.

And it was the obvious rapport between Jenna and Cricket.

Although...

Although he could sense his sister-in-law's alertness, the way her gaze shifted between the two of them, and then fell on his old Trinity Falls athletic t-shirt that she wore.

He longed to stand up and yell that nothing was happening between them.

But you want something to be happening. You want it badly enough that you called her brother today, even if you couldn't find a way to say the words to him.

Jenna loved him like a sister, he knew that. He knew she wanted him to be happy.

But surely telling her honestly that he was falling for

another woman, a woman who wasn't her twin, would be too much to ask her to bear.

And if she knew and couldn't forgive him, he would risk her drifting out of the children's lives. She was the closest thing they all had to Lou. And she was a force of nature all her own, able to make them weep with laughter or stop to consider more serious topics.

"Well, I've got to deliver these two to their grandmother to make cookies," Shane said. "Are you guys ready?"

"Yes," Rumor yelled.

"Yeah, but are you sure you don't need help with the horses?" Wyatt asked.

"Very sure, son," Shane told him, feeling guilty for all the times the boy had helped him when he would have been happier doing kitchen experiments. Why hadn't he ever spoken up?

"I'll walk them over," Cricket offered. "I'm sure you two want to catch up."

There was no point prolonging the inevitable. He would have to talk to Jenna eventually, might as well be now.

"That would be great," he told her. "Thank you."

He watched as she and the kids carried their plates to the sink and scurried off down the hallway to bundle up.

Jenna waited until the door closed behind them before she spoke.

"She's lovely," she said softly.

"Cr... Natalie has been a lifesaver with the kids," he said.

He'd been thinking about her less and less as little Cricket Bell lately, and more like the woman she'd turned into. She wasn't just his best friend's little sister anymore. She was Natalie, and she was more than he'd ever expected.

"That's not what I meant."

Her dark eyes were serious, the usual mischief that sparked there was muted.

It was impossible not to think of Lou when he studied her this way, even though he would never have mistaken one twin for the other, he knew them both too well for that.

Instead of answering, he stood and walked over to the window that looked out over the farm.

The life out there waxed and waned, blooming and withering year after year, as if nothing had changed, though all the time since he had lost Lou had felt like an endless winter.

With Natalie here, he couldn't deny that he could feel tender buds appearing on the tired branches of his soul.

After a moment, Jenna got up and joined him.

"It's been years, Shane," she murmured.

"I could never replace your sister," he said more loudly than he meant to. "Not ever. And I wouldn't want to, even if I could."

"I know that," she said.

"She meant everything to me," he told her, the words choked by an awful sob that seemed to split his chest. "No one could ever replace her, *no one*."

"Shane," she said, moving closer and wrapping an arm around his waist. "Did I ever tell you about my last conversation with Lou?"

He shook his head, feeling broken.

"She always had the best advice," Jenna said, sighing.

He nodded.

"Anyway, it was right after Rich and I broke up," Jenna went on. "You know I held out hope for that guy, in spite of all the evidence we were exactly wrong for each other."

Shane chuckled. He remembered Rich, a humorless

accountant from Philly, who endlessly cleared his throat. He was too boring for Jenna by a mile.

"You're going to do so much better," he told her.

"That's what Lou said," she said with a fond smile. "She said I was better off on my own."

"She was right," he chuckled.

"She always was," Jenna agreed. "Good head on her shoulders, that one, except when it came to her taste in movies."

Shane laughed, picturing his wife sequestered in the bedroom, watching one old school horror movie after another whenever she was home with a cold.

"But she said something else to me that day," Jenna said seriously. "Something I think you might need to hear."

"I'm listening," Shane said.

"She told me it was okay to be sad," Jenna said, turning to him, gazing up at him with her lovely dark eyes. "Even if Rich wasn't the one, it was okay to mourn what I dreamed our future would look like. She said I could be really, really sad, and that no one could tell me not to."

Shane nodded.

"But," Jenna went on, "she also said that one day I would wake up ready to get back to my life. And when that day came, I had to let go. *Life is for living, Jenna,* she said. *You'll have to let go then, because life is for living.*"

He heard the words in Lou's voice, loud and clear, echoing through his mind like bells.

Tears burned his eyes again.

"But I don't want to forget her," he heard himself croak.

"Do you hear yourself?" Jenna asked, blinking through her own tears. "Is there *anything* that would *ever* make you forget her? Even if you wanted to? Can you even *imagine*?"

He shook his head.

"Of course you can't," Jenna said, wiping tears from her own cheeks.

"I miss her so much," he said brokenly.

Jenna went up on her toes and wrapped her wiry, strong arms around him.

"Me too," she whispered.

He hugged her back, and they clung to each other, letting the tears fall for the woman they both would miss.

When they pulled apart, Jenna was smiling up at him fondly.

"Feel better?" she asked.

"Yeah," he said. "You?"

"Yeah," she told him. "Now you just have to figure out how to get your girl. She's a good egg, and the kids obviously adore her. Don't let her get away."

27

NATALIE

Natalie had the kids out the front door and halfway down the porch steps on their way to their grandparents' house to bake cookies, when she realized Rumor didn't have her mittens.

"Stay right here guys," she said. "I'll just pop back in and grab them."

The front door opened easily, and she was in the entryway, grabbing the mittens from the hall table when she heard it.

"I could never replace your sister," Shane was saying, emotion dragging his voice deeper and raspier than usual. "Not ever. And I wouldn't want to even if I could."

Natalie froze in place, mittens in hand.

Jenna said something softly in reply.

"She meant everything to me," Shane said, his voice breaking. "No one could ever replace her, *no one*."

Natalie slipped back out the front door, closing it behind her as quietly as possible, her heart pounding.

"My mittens," Rumor said happily.

Natalie walked down the steps and handed over the

mittens on autopilot.

The cold wind whipped at her face and hair. She was glad for it, because it was an excuse for the red on her cheeks and the tears brimming in her eyes.

"You okay?" Wyatt asked her.

"Yes, of course," she said. "It's just so windy."

"Let's go," Rumor squealed, excited to go eat cookies and read stories.

"Of course," Natalie said. "Hold my hand."

She was pretty sure they were safe from most of the tourist traffic back here near the houses and the red barn, but she couldn't be too safe.

It's not your fault, she told herself. *We don't get to choose who we're attracted to, or who we care about. But we do get to choose what we do about it.*

But that idea was heartbreaking. Because she knew herself too well to think that she would be able to resist Shane's advances if he ever made them.

And knowing that he didn't want to be attracted to her, didn't want to dishonor Lou's memory, meant that if she *really* cared about him, she had to remove the temptation.

Her mind began spinning scenarios immediately. She could move out now, try to find another job, and just get out of their lives.

But the truth was that Shane *did* need her, and the kids needed her. His own mother was relying on her to run errands.

And it wasn't exactly like she had any other job prospects. The money from this gig was paying the taxes on the house.

Maybe she could just keep working for Shane while somehow avoiding his company.

He was out of the house and working in the mornings by

the time she woke Rumor to get ready for school. Avoiding him in the beginning of the day wasn't a problem.

If she came straight back after dropping Rumor off, and made a lunch that could be packed up, she could take Rumor to the park every day after school to avoid seeing him at lunchtime. She could even leave a portion for him.

The only trouble was the afternoons. There was no way to avoid Shane when he came home. She would definitely be preparing dinner with the kids.

But that didn't mean she couldn't excuse herself as soon as he came in and got settled. She could always head back to Nana's place to eat dinner and work on the house.

Shane was early to bed and early to rise, so as long as she didn't come back to the farm until after nine, he would be asleep by the time she came in.

The plan began to solidify in her mind as they approached the big Victorian farmhouse. When they got a little closer, she saw that Mrs. Cassidy was standing out on the porch, ready to welcome the kids inside.

Natalie felt an intense sense of relief that she wouldn't have to go inside and make small talk.

"Who wants hot apple cider?" Mrs. Cassidy yelled to the kids.

"Me," Rumor yelled back, waving with the hand Natalie wasn't holding.

Wyatt waved and grinned at her.

"You'll have cider with us too, right Natalie?" Mrs. Cassidy asked as they approached.

"I can't today," Natalie told her. "I've been avoiding Nana's house, but I definitely need to get over there and keep sorting through things. Thank you for the offer, though."

"Stay right there," Mrs. Cassidy said, dashing back into

the house.

Natalie looked over at Wyatt, who was smiling and shaking his head.

"What?" she asked.

"She's fixing you one to go," he told her.

Sure enough, Mrs. Cassidy jogged out to the porch with a lidded ceramic tumbler.

"Take this with you," she recommended. "It'll keep you warm in the car, and give you a little energy for a difficult task."

"Thank you," Natalie said over a lump in her throat, stepping up to take it.

The tumbler was warm in her hand.

"Are you all right, dear?" Mrs. Cassidy asked quietly, searching her face with concern.

"It's just the wind," Natalie lied. "I'm fine."

"I see," Mrs. Cassidy said. "Well, thank you for bringing the kids over. I'm sure we'll see each other soon."

"Absolutely," Natalie told her. "I'll be running errands on Monday, don't you worry."

"You're an angel," Mrs. Cassidy told her.

She raised her cider as if in a salute and jogged back down the steps before anyone could make her cry by saying one more kind word.

When she arrived back at Shane's place, she remembered that she didn't have her own car.

Thankfully, the keys to the truck were still in her jacket pocket. She got in, and the engine started with a mighty roar.

She tried not to look at the house and think about what Shane and Jenna might be talking about.

As soon as I get back to Nana's, I'll feel better. When I get home, I'll feel like myself.

28

SHANE

Shane paced back and forth in front of the living room sofa.

His emotions stormed endlessly today. Tears had splashed from his eyes more than once, rumbles of fear rolled in his belly, and flashes of the happiness they might all have together, if he had the courage to take the next steps, illuminated his heart from time to time, keeping him focused on what he had to do.

Kids first, then Natalie, he told himself. *Just two more hurdles between the present and the future.*

Jenna had set off with the kids on a hike through the farm trails when the last batch of cookies was in the oven. That had allowed him to sit with his parents and talk everything over with them.

His mom had cried when he told her how he felt. His dad nodded at him, a proud, assessing expression on his face, for once his joking set aside to celebrate something solemn and wonderful.

Of course, they both gave their blessing right away.

He just wasn't sure how the kids would react.

They both adored Natalie. That much was clear. But it was one thing to love your nanny, and another to feel that she was going to take your mother's place.

Rumor was still so small, but Wyatt was a teenager, with all the complicated feelings that went along with such a big transition from childhood to being a young adult.

And Shane hardly had enough time with them as things were. Would they want to share what was left of his time with someone else?

He heard the front door burst open. then Rumor's light footsteps pattering toward him.

"Hey guys," he said, turning to greet them.

Their eyes were shining, and their cheeks were pink from the cold, but they looked happy.

"I'm just going to head back to your parents to make sure they don't need anything," Jenna said, giving him a quick salute.

"Thanks, sis," he said, wishing she could stay and share her infectious enthusiasm and positive thinking with them.

But this was his alone to do.

"Let me help you with your coat," he laughed, watching Rumor try to wrestle herself out without removing her mittens. "Wyatt, stick around for a minute, okay? I wanted to chat with you guys about something."

"Sure," Wyatt said, kicking off his boots.

"I have to pee," Rumor announced as soon as she was free of her snow pants.

"Okay," Shane said. "Run and do that and then meet Wyatt and me in the living room."

She trundled off obediently, and he turned and headed into the living room, where Wyatt was already sprawled on the sofa.

"You guys had fun?" Shane guessed with a smile.

"We always have fun with Aunt Jenna," Wyatt said returning the smile. "She's hilarious."

Shane nodded, biting back the conversation he knew they needed to have until Rumor could return.

"This is about Natalie, isn't it?" Wyatt asked suddenly.

"How did you know?" Shane asked, lowering himself into his favorite chair in relief.

"Seems like you guys like each other," Wyatt said with a shrug.

"How do you feel about that?" Shane asked.

Wyatt frowned in thought.

Shane felt his heart quiver. Nothing came before his kids. Nothing. If Wyatt didn't want this, it wouldn't happen. Period.

"I thinks it's cool," Wyatt said at last.

Shane blinked at him, unable to process.

"What's cool, Wyatt?" Rumor asked, scrambling up on the sofa beside him and snuggling her little body into her brother's.

"Do you want to tell her, or should I?" Wyatt asked, wrapping an arm around her.

"I can do it," Shane told his son with a smile.

"What?" Rumor demanded. "What? What? What?"

"Dad likes Natalie," Wyatt said, spilling the beans himself anyway.

"Me too," Rumor decided. "She's nice."

"No, Rumor, he *like*-likes her," Wyatt said.

She looked up at her brother and then across at her father.

"I like-like her too," she crowed. "I like-like-*love* her. She took me to the park and put chips on my sandwich and they were *crunchy*."

"I give up," Wyatt said.

But Shane was laughing too hard to tackle it on his own.

"Do you want Dad to marry her?" Wyatt asked his sister, trying a new tack.

Rumor's expression turned serious.

"Will she turn into a frog?" she asked cautiously.

"Definitely not," Wyatt told her.

"Princess Tiana turned into a frog," Rumor reminded him.

"No," Wyatt told her. "Princess Tiana turned back into a person when she got married, remember? And besides, turning into a frog is very... unlikely."

Shane smiled, glad to see Wyatt trying to take his sister's concerns seriously.

"Kids," he said, leaning forward. "No one is getting married right now. But if Natalie and I were dating, it would mean that I went out with her in the evenings sometimes, just the two of us. Would that be okay with you, if I asked her on a date?"

"Of course," Wyatt said.

"Will she still have time to take me to the park?" Rumor asked worriedly.

"Yes," Shane said. "I don't think she would ever want to miss out on any of her time with you."

"Okay," Rumor said, sliding off the couch and heading for her box of blocks as if the matter were settled.

Shane watched his daughter in awe. She was so resilient. Wyatt cleared his throat and Shane turned back to see that he had a pensive look on his face.

"I could never replace your mom," Shane said quietly to him. "You know that right?"

"I know, Dad," Wyatt said.

Shane thought about the baking and the work on the farm, and how his son hadn't shared his feelings out of a sense of wanting to be helpful. He couldn't risk that happening again.

"If there was something you wanted or were worried about, I hope you would trust me enough to tell me," Shane said. "I want that more than I want anything else we've talked about tonight."

"You haven't gone on dates before," Wyatt said. "Since Mom, right?"

"No," Shane said. "You're right. I haven't."

"I'll bet you wish you had now," Wyatt said.

"Why's that?" Shane asked, feeling lost.

"I was just thinking that it would be better to practice on someone we don't all like so much," Wyatt said.

"You think I'm going to mess it up, huh?" Shane asked, trying not to laugh again. The kid probably had a darned good point.

"Nah," Wyatt said, grinning at him. "You'll get it right. Besides, she's pretty patient."

Shane thought to himself that if she was half as patient and accepting as his kids, he couldn't possibly mess it up.

"Can I make hot chocolate?" Wyatt asked.

"Sure," Shane told him.

As Rumor built a tower of blocks, and Wyatt hummed to himself in the kitchen, Shane felt the tender buds on the branches of his heart begin to unfurl in the light.

29

NATALIE

Natalie straightened up, stretching her back for a minute and pushing the hair that had fallen out of her ponytail behind her ears.

She had spent the day feeling shipwrecked, with her heart aching and her spirit stranded on some far away island.

But looking around Nana's garage, she was surprised to feel a tiny spark of encouragement.

She might be physically tired, covered in dust and steeped in memories, but she was starting to see actual progress.

See, all you have to do is get your heart broken, and you'll do anything to distract yourself.

There were boxes of recycling filled with old newspapers, bottles, and plastic. Next, came stacks of boxes of things that could go to the church thrift shop to be considered for sale to benefit charity. Those boxes finally included almost all of Nana's clothing, something that had been too tough to sort through until today.

There was even a small pile of papers that she thought should probably be shredded.

The house was still nowhere near ready to go on the market. But it was certainly starting to look much more streamlined inside, and even the garage staging area had a method to its madness.

"Natalie?" a familiar voice called out.

For once, instead of feeling embarrassed, she was excited to hear her real estate agent's voice.

"Hey, Sloane," she said, turning to see the other woman heading up the drive. "How's it going?"

"I was just taking my walk," Sloane said. "Look how organized you are."

Sloane Greenfield was the top producer at Trinity Falls Realty Group. Unlike the real estate agents in the movies, with their big hair and fancy cars, Sloane drove an ancient silver Volvo, and her long brown hair hung straight down her back, in keeping with her endless collection of long plaid skirts, riding boots, and modest sweaters.

To Natalie, she looked less like a real estate agent than she did the young headmistress of an English day school.

Sloane prepped her listing clients like a headmistress too, liberal with the carrot, but unafraid to use the stick, as needed.

"I got a job, but now that it's the weekend, I'm trying to really get stuff done here," Natalie told her proudly.

"Sometimes, the more you have to do, the better you manage your time," Sloane said. "That's definitely the case for me in the springtime."

"Well, it will probably be springtime before this place is ready for the market," Natalie said. "But I'm making progress."

"Want to show it off?" Sloane asked, waggling her eyebrows comically.

"Sure," Natalie laughed. "Just don't get your hopes up."

She headed into the house with Sloane trailing after her.

Just a minute ago, Natalie had been feeling proud of how much she had accomplished. Now, she suddenly began seeing the place through Sloane's eyes. There were still too many books on the shelves, and doilies on the tabletops, and she hadn't removed a single ceramic pig.

"There's still a ton of stuff," she said apologetically. "And obviously, I haven't gotten any of the wallpaper down or painting done. That's going to have to wait until the rewiring is finished."

But Sloane was pacing through the living room, looking thoughtfully at the space.

"Couple of thoughts," Sloane said. "First of all, remember in the very beginning, we said you could sell the house as-is, since the market was strong?"

Natalie nodded.

"Well, it's stronger now than it was when we had that talk," Sloane said. "And that's just in general. Trinity Falls, specifically, has a market that's going a little gaga because of the highway coming in. One possibility if you sell as-is would be someone who would plan to gut the place and renovate anyway. I know it's sad to think about, but on the positive side, it might mean you don't even have to empty the place out."

Natalie nodded, trying not to think about what the wild market and desirability of the town was going to do to the rental market she would be competing in as soon as she sold this place.

"The other possibility has to do with zoning," Sloane

said, her dark eyes sparkling with the idea. "This block is zoned commercial as well as residential."

"That can't be right," Natalie said.

"Old Mr. Beldorph didn't want the block to turn commercial," Sloane said, shaking her head. "Back in the day, he made a gentlemen's agreement with his neighbors that none of them would sell to a consortium that was trying to buy up commercial space in town at the time. They stood by that and none of them sold, no matter the price. Since then, there hasn't been enough demand for commercial space to tempt anyone. But times have changed."

"What would someone even put here?" Natalie asked, trying to image the bungalow as something different.

"Oh, maybe someone will buy it and turn it into one of those cute boutique coffee shops," Sloane said excitedly.

Natalie wrinkled her nose.

"Sorry," Sloane said immediately. "I didn't mean to bring up a sore subject."

She meant the viral video that was buzzing of Natalie knocking herself and Holly over to the *Wipe Out* song.

But that wasn't what had made Natalie wince, not at all.

The last thing this town needs is another trendy coffee shop.

Mr. Cassidy's words echoed in her head. He was right. They already had good coffee in town.

But there was one thing the town didn't have.

"I've got it," she said suddenly, like a scientist yelling *Eureka*.

Looking around, she could picture it perfectly. And the reason it was easy to picture was that the home had been used as a gathering place by her Nana for as long as she could remember.

"What is it?" Sloane asked with a smile.

"What if I could make the first floor into a gathering

place for older people?" Natalie asked. "A place where they could come and drink coffee and play board games and gossip?"

"This town could use a place like that," Sloane said thoughtfully. "Though I don't know that there's much money in it. It could be hard to sell that concept to an investor."

"What if I wanted to hang onto the place?" Natalie asked. "I could do it myself, right?"

"We'd have to talk to the borough," Sloane said, immediately sliding out her phone. "I'm going to send you a link to the building and zoning codes, so you can just start reading them over."

Natalie felt her phone buzz in her pocket.

"Would you be looking to earn a living out of this?" Sloane asked her plainly.

"I know that's not reasonable," Natalie said, shaking her head. "I'd want to make the upstairs into an apartment for myself so I wouldn't have to rent a place. And I'd need to make sure the costs were covered."

"If you had non-profit status, you could probably do that with donations," Sloane said. "I think this could be something people in town would want to support. I'll talk to another client of mine. He's an attorney, and he might be able to walk you through what that would entail. Maybe even offer you a few hours pro bono."

Natalie's phone buzzed again, and she smiled.

"I'll have to talk to my brother," she said. "He's entitled to half the proceeds of the sale. But his service is going well, and I think he might like this idea."

"Well, no pressure, but I love it," Sloane said. "I'm glad to help you with any connections you need if this is the route you and Chris choose."

"I really appreciate it," Natalie said, suddenly realizing that Sloane wouldn't be paid for any of her work if she didn't actually sell the house.

"What?" Sloane asked.

"I was just thinking," Natalie said. "I mean, you've been working with me for months already."

"Don't you worry about me," Sloane said with a smile. "This town has always been good to me. *Do the right thing, and the money will follow,* that's what my mentor used to say, and he was right. I really like this idea, Natalie, it feels like it could be the right thing for you, and it would definitely be great for Trinity Falls."

Natalie found herself wrapping her arms around her surprised agent and giving her a grateful hug.

This day might not be turning out the way she planned, but the promise of something good on the horizon made her feel a little bit more like herself again.

30

SHANE

Shane paced worriedly in the hallway as Rumor chose which of her stuffed animals would sleep in her bed with her.

He wasn't sure when he had expected Natalie to come home, but it definitely wasn't this late.

On a whim, he slipped his phone out of his pocket and sent her a quick text.

ME:

Hey, just wanted to make sure you're ok. Hope your day was productive.

HE WATCHED the screen for a moment, but there was no response.

"I'm ready for my story," Rumor called to him.

He headed into her room and smiled when he saw which book she had chosen.

"*The Princess and the Frog*, huh?" he asked.

"I like that one," she said, grinning.

He sat beside her and read to her until her eyelashes were kissing her cheeks. Then he tucked the blanket around her and turned off the lamp.

As he walked down the hall, he saw that the light was off in Wyatt's room, too. The hike with Jenna must have worn them both out.

He made it all the way downstairs before checking his phone again.

There was still no response from Natalie.

He ran a hand through his hair and tried to decide what to do. He couldn't just show up at her Nana's house. And besides, the kids were in bed.

He decided to give it another half an hour. To kill the time, he would bring in the Christmas tree he had cut earlier. He'd dragged it up on the porch this afternoon, but it needed to come in and get set up.

He pulled on a pair of work gloves and headed out, propping the doors open.

It was a frigid but beautiful night. The air was cold and sweet, and the starlight reflected on the snowy ground. It was a perfect night to sit on the front porch under a blanket with mugs of hot apple cider.

Stop thinking about her.

But it was no use. He checked his phone again. Still nothing, though this time it looked like she had seen his message.

He sighed in relief. So at least she wasn't in a ditch somewhere.

He'd been itching to call his brother, but that wasn't necessary. It was good to have family in law enforcement, but now that Cal was sheriff, it felt weird to pull strings.

He started dragging the tree toward the doors, scowling at the idea that he might be scuffing the painted porch floor.

He hadn't always had to bring the tree in by himself. He'd been hoping this year maybe Natalie would help.

Visions had swirled in his head of her decorating the tree with him and the kids, drinking eggnog, playing holiday music - whatever she wanted.

He had been coming around to the idea of a Christmas with some new traditions, not just trying to breathe life back into the old ones and always coming up short.

"What in the world are you doing?" Jenna's voice rang out in the cold night air.

"What does it look like?" he chuckled.

"I guess I should have said, *Why are you doing it alone?*" she said, jogging up the steps and heading to one end of the tree.

"I've been doing it alone for years," he said, shrugging.

"*Why?*" she asked. "I get it that Lou isn't here, but you have friends, family, heck, even Wyatt could help you now."

"I don't like asking for help," he heard himself admit.

"Well, you might not *like* it," she said. "But you have to let people help you anyway. You know that's all anyone ever wants, right?"

He shrugged.

There was one person whose help he hadn't instinctively pushed away. One person who was currently ignoring him.

"Come on," Jenna said bending to grab the top of the tree. "Let's do this."

But his phone finally chirped.

"Hang on," he said, grabbing it out of his pocket.

She nodded and straightened up.

. . .

CRICKET:

Got a lot done. I'm staying here for the night so I can get more done tomorrow.

HE HELD the phone to his chest and closed his eyes, a sinking sensation making him feel as if he were falling through the porch floor and into the ground.

"What?" Jenna asked worriedly. "Is everything okay?"

"She's staying at her Nana's house tonight," he said quietly. "She says she wants to get more work done there tomorrow."

"Okay," Jenna said. "That's too bad. I know you wanted to talk to her."

It was more than that, but he didn't know how to tell her that he felt like his stomach was full of lead.

"Are you freaking out?" she asked.

"Did I scare her away?" he wondered out loud.

"Wait," Jenna said. "Wait, wait, wait. You haven't even asked her out yet, right?"

He nodded.

"So how can you be scaring her away?" Jenna asked.

"I don't know," he said, shaking his head and feeling stupid. "I just have this bad feeling."

"You have a bad feeling because you're nervous," Jenna guessed. "You haven't asked anyone out since high school. But it's good that she's cleaning out her grandmother's house. She'll feel less stressed out when that's taken care of."

"You're right," he said, nodding. "I've been talking about this all day with everyone I love, but for her I guess it's just a normal day."

"Psychopath," Jenna muttered.

"What?" he asked, grinning.

"Nothing," she said.

"I distinctly heard someone say *psychopath*," he said.

"Well, it couldn't have been me," she replied. "I personally think it's completely normal for you to wig out and ask your entire family for their blessing when she hasn't even said if she likes you back or not."

He winced.

"I'm kidding, Shane," she said. "She obviously likes you. Everyone knows it. She can barely look at you."

"That doesn't seem like good evidence," he said. "Maybe she just doesn't like how I look."

"And now he's fishing for compliments," Jenna told her invisible audience. "Just grab the trunk, Romeo. Let's get this thing inside."

He did as he was told, and tried to ignore the pit in his stomach.

He was grateful to have family around to keep his head on straight.

31

NATALIE

On Monday evening, Natalie stood in the kitchen, prepping a salad with Wyatt while a lasagna baked in the oven.

Even after a weekend of focusing on her future, and a day of fun with Rumor and Wyatt, she was still nervous about seeing Shane again for the first time since she'd made up her mind about him.

Luckily, with Sloane's help, she had a plan for this evening that would get her out the door just about as soon as he came in. So, she didn't have to stay strong for long.

As if she had summoned him with a thought, the front door opened.

"Daddy," Rumor yelled, trucking down the hall to greet him, book still in hand.

"Hey, sunshine," he said, scooping her up.

Natalie dragged her eyes back to the salad in front of her.

"Hey, Wyatt," Shane said as he strode into the kitchen with Rumor in his arms. "Something smells good."

"We made a lasagna," Wyatt said proudly.

"That's amazing," Shane said. "I can't wait to sit down and eat, and hear about everyone's day."

His eyes sought Natalie's and her heart sank at his sweet, hopeful expression.

She wished she could have a nice meal with the family again, and maybe she could one day. But for now, it was just too hard not to let her feelings run away with her imagination.

Whether he seemed to be attracted to her or not, she had heard what he said to Jenna loud and clear. He didn't *want* to replace his wife.

The least Natalie could do was honor that.

"Actually, I've got something going on tonight," she said carefully. "I have to pop out as soon as you're settled in."

"What's going on?" he asked.

"Natalie has a plan to turn her Nana's house into a gathering spot for seniors," Wyatt said.

"Really?" Shane asked. "I thought you were going to sell."

"I was talking with Sloane Greenfield on Saturday, and the idea just materialized," Natalie said. "She told me she thought it could work, and we've been brainstorming how to do it ever since. Chris texted me to give his blessing yesterday."

"That's really amazing," Shane said.

There was warmth in his voice that made blood rush to her cheeks.

"So, are you going to meet with Sloane now?" he asked.

"Actually, I'm doing something I kind of can't believe I would ever do," she admitted.

"She's meeting a *reporter*," Wyatt said excitedly. "From the news station."

"No way," Shane said. "You're a mover and a shaker. An interview after only three days of brainstorming?"

"Well," Natalie said, feeling embarrassed. "They wanted to interview me anyway. I was going to say no, but then I asked if they would highlight my project and they said yes."

"Ah, big city musician comes back to her hometown," Shane said, nodding.

Wyatt started laughing and the embarrassed feeling in Natalie's chest ebbed a little.

"It's actually about the buzz from my, um, entertaining incident at Jolly Beans," she admitted sheepishly.

"Oh, wow," he said, looking impressed. "You're willing to draw more attention to it?"

"It's for a good cause," she said, shrugging.

"Dad, like two million people have seen it," Wyatt said. "Sharing it with our little town paper won't change anything."

Natalie smiled fondly at him. Of course, Wyatt might see it that way, but for her it was different.

Most of the two million people who might have seen the video were strangers. Just about everyone, old and young, who had known Natalie and her family since childhood watched the local news channel.

But her total humiliation would be worth it, if it meant Nana's house could be transformed into something worthy of her memory.

"I think it's very brave," Shane said. "And you can head out now, if you want. We can take it from here."

"I'm off," Natalie said quickly, jogging down the hall to retrieve her coat.

"Natalie, you're coming back, right?" Rumor piped up suddenly, trotting down the hall after her.

"Of course I'm coming back," Natalie told her, crouching

so the little one could see her face easily. "I'll wake you up in the morning, like always."

Rumor gave her a big hug, and she felt her heart ache just a little.

32

NATALIE

Half an hour later, Natalie was sitting at the best table in Jolly Beans, a mug of tea clutched in her hands.

Honey Peterson of Channel 12 news sat across from her, sipping a peppermint mocha latte.

The cameraman was set up to the right of them, in order to get a shot of both women and the big glass window with Trinity Falls village decked out in its wintry best behind them.

"My editor is so impressed that you're doing this," Honey said with a wink. "It's one thing to know people are reliving your most embarrassing moment on an app. It's another thing to talk about it to your hometown news channel."

"It's pretty mortifying," Natalie agreed, nodding. "But I'm hoping I can turn it around to support a good cause."

"Very admirable," Honey said. "So, let's talk about it. What were you doing here at Jolly Beans that day?"

"I had come to apply for a job waiting tables, believe it or not," Natalie said, shaking her head. "A good friend of mine is a waitress here, and she said it's a great place to work."

"Is that..." Honey said, checking her tablet, "Holly Fields?"

"Yes, that's her," Natalie said.

"Okay," Honey said. "So, what happened?"

"Well, there's not much to it," Natalie said. "I got here and the owner, Pete, was in the back preparing a huge order of food. So, I was waiting for him to be free to talk with me. I thought he was beckoning me over, but he was waving to Holly, who was carrying a massive tray of food. When I moved towards him, so did she, and I knocked into her."

"You two hit the ground pretty hard," Honey said. "Was anyone injured?"

"Just my pride," Natalie said. "And of course, all that food was wasted, and the customers had to wait for more to be prepared."

"Then what happened?" Honey asked.

"Surprisingly, I didn't get the job," Natalie laughed. "But I did land another one though, so no one needs to worry about me."

"I think you left something out," Honey said, lifting an eyebrow.

"What?" Natalie asked.

"One thing a lot of viewers are noticing about that video is the way the owner of Jolly Beans, Pete Anderson, spoke to you after the incident," Honey said. "Would you agree that his words and tone were cruel and dismissive?"

"I can't help but put myself in Pete's shoes," Natalie said carefully. "This is a small café, and that was such a big order that the whole staff was helping to prepare and serve it. I feel terrible thinking about how much time and food was wasted because of me. In that moment, I'm sure any one of us would have lost our patience."

"But he lost control," Honey said, as if hoping she could get Natalie to admit to something different. "Some people are even talking about boycotting this place."

"I don't think he lost control," Natalie said firmly. "What he said wasn't friendly, but it was accurate. And he didn't use foul language or personal insults. Again, I think the average person in that situation would be upset, too. Pete's a good guy and he runs a lovely establishment. I would be really sad to see Trinity Falls lose this place. It's definitely one of my favorite hangouts."

"That's why you insisted on being interviewed here?" Honey asked.

Natalie nodded.

Pete finally looked up at her from his place behind the counter. When they had arrived, he'd been hiding in the back.

The man was obviously embarrassed for lashing out the other day.

He gave her a cautious smile now, and mouthed the words *thank you*.

She smiled back and then returned her attention to Honey.

"So, why did you want to be a waitress?" Honey asked.

"I waited tables in New York before I came back to Trinity Falls," Natalie said.

"You were there to pursue a music career?" Honey asked.

"It didn't work out the way I had hoped," Natalie admitted.

"Was there a reason for your timing in returning home?" Honey asked.

"My Nana, who raised me, was ill," Natalie said, willing herself not to get teary. "She recently passed away. Now I want to do something to honor her memory."

"And that's why you agreed to this interview in the first place?" Honey asked.

"I'm obviously really, really embarrassed about that video," Natalie said. "And I know your show is super popular. If anyone I know didn't already see the BeeBop, they're definitely going to now."

Honey laughed, looking pleased.

"But I'm hoping they might also agree to help me out with the project in some way," Natalie went on.

"Can you tell us about it?" Honey asked.

"It's pretty simple, really," Natalie said. "My grandmother's bungalow is just a block from the shops here on Park Avenue. She spent her life hosting parties and get-togethers there. I'd like to turn it into a gathering place where retirees like she was can swing by to hang out, play board games, and pass the time with some company."

"What will that take?" Honey asked, leaning forward.

"Well, there are the legal and technical requirements with the borough," Natalie said. "My angel of a real estate agent, Sloane Greenfield from Trinity Falls Realty Group, is donating her time and expertise to help me navigate that."

"Wonderful," Honey said, nodding.

"And then I'd like to get the place ADA compliant," Natalie said. "That will mean making some renovations - adding a ramp and widening doorways, and probably some things I haven't thought of yet."

"What can people do, if they're interested in helping?" Honey asked.

"Of course, if anyone with expertise in construction

wants to generously donate advice, labor, materials or any combination of the three we would be very grateful," Natalie said.

"What about the rest of us?" Honey asked.

"I'll be hosting a Beef & Beer at the firehouse to raise funds," Natalie said. "If anyone wants to come out for a delicious meal, music, dancing and to support a great cause, I'd be so happy to see you there."

"I wouldn't miss it for the world," Honey said, smiling. "We've got the info up on the screen for everyone now, or you can check out the station's BeeBop pinned post, if you don't have a pen handy."

"Thank you," Natalie said, impressed.

"Thank *you*, for speaking with us," Honey said. "Natalie Bell, a clumsy woman with a graceful heart. Meet her in person at the firehouse this Saturday at seven."

Honey hopped up and offered her hand, which Natalie took, shaking it firmly.

"That was really great," Honey said. "People will love it. You were very natural."

"Uh, thanks," Natalie said.

"Come on, Howie," Honey said. "We're off to a skating rink in Upper Shire now."

They packed up and bustled out quickly, leaving Natalie to shove her notes into her backpack and carry her mug to the counter.

"Natalie," Pete said softly, coming out from behind the counter. "I'm so sorry for the way I spoke to you."

"And I'm still very sorry for ruining all those lunches," Natalie said.

"What you did today was more than I deserve," he said, gesturing to the film crew getting into the car out front. "I know you said you got another job, but if you ever want to work here, you have an open offer."

"Thank you," she said with feeling.

"And I'd like to donate all the desserts for your fundraiser," he said. "Just let me know when you have an idea of head count, and I'll make sure you have more than you need."

"Pete, that's too generous," she said, awed. "I can't let you do it."

"Try and stop me," he joked weakly. "Seriously though, Natalie, it will ease my guilt a little. And if you're willing to have me, I'll be there to serve, too."

Natalie grabbed his hands in hers, went up on her toes and kissed his cheek.

"This means the world to me, Pete," she told him, pulling back without letting go of his hands. "I'm sorry all this happened, but I'm starting to think that a lot of good might come out of it."

He squeezed her hands back and smiled at her for real this time, until his eyes crinkled.

"Shane Cassidy's a lucky man," he said, shaking his head. "You've got a heart of gold, kid."

For a moment she thought he must think she and Shane were together. Then she realized that of course he was just referring to the fact that she was watching Shane's kids.

Her heart ached with sudden sadness, but there was no way she was letting that out in the open.

"I feel lucky to spend time with him and the kids," she said with a big smile, letting go of his hands. "I have to run, but I'll see you later, Pete."

"See you at the firehouse," he called after her. "But don't forget to text me when you have an idea on how many people."

"Will do," she said.

She managed to open the door and step out into the cold winter night before the tears prickled her eyes.

What are you moping about? she scolded herself inwardly. *You're doing something important, finally, something meaningful.*

33

SHANE

Shane straightened his tie for the fifth time and tugged on his jacket. Though he was no stranger to looking nice for church or school gatherings, it had been a while since an event had been so important to someone he cared about.

And if he was honest with himself, he was nervous about tonight.

For the past week, Natalie had been wrapped up in her project from the moment he got home each afternoon until after he was in bed.

He knew it was important to her, and he expected nothing less of the hardworking and dedicated young woman he had gotten to know lately.

But he couldn't help but also assume that any attraction she felt for him had cooled, if she had even thought of him that way in the first place. She'd barely spared him a second glance.

If she felt about him the way he did about her, she would be thinking about him throughout the day, wanting to send messages asking how the day was going, sharing the struggles and triumphs of her life with him.

She obviously didn't share his feelings, but he was pretty sure she suspected his. That was the other reason she was always scurrying away the minute he came in the door. She probably didn't want to lead him on.

I'm going to show her that I understand, he told himself as he clapped his best cowboy hat on his head. *I'm going to make sure she sees that I know how to be just-friends, and that I'll do it for her. I'll do anything for her, even if it hurts.*

The hardest thing he'd done so far was talk to the kids again and explain that he wasn't going to ask Natalie to go on a date after all.

Rumor had been heartbroken, but Wyatt just nodded coolly, like he was disappointed, but wasn't going to waste his breath.

"It's important that we honor people's choices when we care about them," he had tried to explain. "I don't want to put Natalie on the spot when it's clear that she's not interested in having me for a boyfriend. It might make her feel sad or embarrassed to have to tell me no, and I would never want that."

"Daddy, I'm a princess," Rumor squealed, snapping him out of his thoughts as she dashed in with the flowing tulle of her green dress hiked up in her little hands.

"Yes, you are," he told her. "You look awesome."

"Wait until Cricket sees me," Rumor said. "She'll want to play princess tea party with me."

"Oh, sweetheart, I'm glad you mentioned that," Shane said, crouching down to pull her into a hug, then releasing her but keeping his hands on her arms. "She's going to be super busy tonight, because she has to run the whole party.

So, we'll get to say hi to her, but she probably won't have time to play."

"She'll play with me tomorrow," Rumor said bravely, but her lower lip pouted out just a little, so he knew she was sad.

"And *I'll* play with you tonight," Shane decided. "We can play princess and cowboy tea party."

"*Ha*," Rumor yelled, tipping her chin up and laughing her head off.

"You guys ready?" Wyatt asked, stepping in.

"Whoa," Shane said.

"What?" Wyatt asked. But his cheeks flushed slightly with pleasure.

He looked great, and he knew it. He was wearing jeans and a white button down with his grandfather's blue velvet blazer.

"You look like a rock star," Shane told him.

"Thanks," Wyatt said, looking very pleased.

"Let's go, let's go," Rumor yelled.

Suddenly, Shane felt a little better. Though he had really hoped to draw Natalie into their little family, things were pretty amazing just as they were.

"I'm the luckiest guy in the world," he realized out loud as he looked at the three of them together in the mirror.

"Okay, lucky guy," Wyatt teased. "Let's go get some food. I'm starving."

34

NATALIE

Natalie glanced around the crowded firehouse and noticed that yet another group of Nana's old friends was about to converge on her.

Happiness flooded her chest, though a tiny corner of her heart remained empty. She had invited Shane and the kids, but she wasn't sure they would actually come.

Things with Shane had been subdued. At first, she had made herself deliberately busy in order to avoid him. But as soon as plans for tonight's event got underway, she found that she was legitimately overwhelmed with things that needed doing.

If she hadn't assembled an amazing crew of friends to help, she was sure tonight never could have happened, especially with such short notice.

Sloane stood by a big table against one wall, overseeing the silent auction where Nana's friends had gathered up donations of homemade quilts, jars of jam, works by local artists, and even offers of handyman tasks to be sold to the highest bidder.

Pete was walking among the tables, making sure

everyone had all they needed for their meal and that the drinks were flowing.

"What a triumph," Betty Ann Eustace declared, wrapping an arm around Natalie's shoulders as her two partners in crime, Shirley Ludd and Ginny Davies joined them, conspiratorial smiles on their faces.

"Thank you so much," Natalie said. "I could never have done it without you."

"You could have," Shirley said.

"But it wouldn't have come out like this," Ginny added proudly. "We're so glad we could help."

"Besides, you know I never could have let Carla's pigs be thrown away," Betty Ann said. "This way everyone can enjoy them."

And those weren't the only things sticking around. The ladies had been helping Natalie decide which things could stay in the house and what should be replaced.

The lumpy sofas would make way for larger, firmer sectionals that were easier to get in and out of. The wooden kitchen table with the coffee rings on it that made Natalie smile remembering the endless cups that had been drunk there would stay, and so would the pig collection. But the old coffeemaker with the replacement carafe that never quite fit would be replaced with a nice new cappuccino machine, if Betty Ann had her say.

"Excuse me," a shy female voice said.

Natalie turned to see a woman about her age, who looked awfully familiar.

"You probably don't remember me," she said. "But I grew up in the apartment building behind your Nana's house. There was a kitchen fire one Christmas Eve, and you all took us in for the night. It could have been awful, and instead, it's one of my favorite childhood memories.

Anyway, my mom wanted me to bring this donation in your Nana's honor and ask me to remind you of that night."

"Charlotte?" Natalie remembered. "Charlotte Kendrick?"

"You *do* remember me," Charlotte said happily.

"We almost hurt ourselves from laughing so hard while we played Uno with Nancy Webb and Erik Undine that night," Natalie said. "How could I ever forget?"

Charlotte pressed the envelope into her hand and Natalie pulled her in for a quick hug.

"Thank you so much," Natalie said. "This would make Nana so happy."

"I'm glad," Charlotte said with a big smile. "I should let you go. You have so many people who want to speak to you."

Charlotte was looking over Natalie's shoulder.

She turned to see Shane and the kids waiting for her, and her stomach did a little flip-flop, like at the top of a roller coaster.

Rumor wore a beautiful, fluffy green princess gown, complete with an understated rhinestone crown. She looked so happy that she was practically quivering.

Wyatt looked handsome and very cool and retro in jeans and a velvet blazer.

And Shane.

Oh, Shane, she thought. *How am I ever supposed to not notice how handsome you are?*

She hadn't seen him so dressed up since the Snow Ball all those years ago. His light cowboy hat contrasted with his dark hair.

"Natalie, everything looks wonderful," he said warmly, removing the hat to greet her.

"Thank you, Shane," she replied. "Thank you for making it easy for me to get this organized. I could never have done this if you'd kept me late as many times as you probably wanted to."

"I would be proud to have any part in this," he said. "But truly, you made it happen from the ground up. I hope you realize how special it is, the gift you have for drawing people in, allowing them to see how much they want to help."

The compliment nearly sank her because she felt the truth of it. Shane *saw* her. She might not be the best guitarist, the best waitress, or even the best nanny. But she had been blessed with an ability to find hidden gifts in the people around her. And by some power greater than her own, encourage them to use those gifts to do something wonderful.

"Time for supper, and I think for a song," Sloane called out in her rich contralto.

"You won't have time for a tea party tonight," Rumor said, tugging on Natalie's skirt.

"You might be right, Rumor," Natalie admitted. "But I *definitely* want you to put that amazing outfit on again tomorrow for a tea party. If it's okay with your Dad."

"Of course," Shane said. "We'll let you get back to it."

A few minutes later the food was served, and she had dropped off the envelopes and folded cash gifts she had received to Sloane, who was counting the donations and entering each onto a spreadsheet in her laptop.

There was nothing for Natalie to do but grab her guitar and head up to the chair on the makeshift stage.

Though she hadn't had much time to practice in the last few weeks, the wooden neck felt like home in her hand, and the music flowed from the strings as if it were self-generating and her only job was to control and channel it.

People turned to watch and listen politely, but after a

few minutes, they turned back to their dining partners to chat.

This was the trouble with Natalie's music. She loved it and it made a fun backdrop. But at the end of the day, she didn't have that star quality that could turn her passion into a career.

Right here, right now, though? It felt just right. Creating a beautiful backdrop for an evening with friends was an honor that was a payment unto itself.

She lost herself in it, letting the songs transition from an old R&B classic into a Christmas carol, and from there into one of her favorite Elvis tunes.

Suddenly, she noticed a flash of movement in the crowd out of the corner of her eye. She looked up from the strings and saw that Wyatt was jogging up onto the stage.

"Can I join you?" he murmured.

"Sure," she said, mystified.

He spun to face the crowd and was instantly transformed, shaking his hips, letting his head fall back to howl out the lyrics and generally becoming his own very young, very hip thirteen-year-old version of The King.

At first there was stunned silence.

Then Betty Ann began to cheer. The others joined her, and within a few minutes the whole place was laughing with surprise and admiration, with most of the crowd singing along with him.

When the song was done, Wyatt's cheeks were flushed with pleasure. He bowed as everyone howled their approval.

Natalie tried to coax him into an encore with the first few bars of another Elvis song and he delighted everyone by obliging.

The whole firehouse was humming with life and Natalie

played her heart out, loving the response she'd never quite had before, no matter how well her gigs had gone.

Is this because it's Wyatt singing, and I adore seeing him feel confident like this?

She was pretty sure it was, but she was playing too hard and having too much fun to worry much about it.

After their third song she glanced over at Sloane, who nodded to her. That meant the donations were counted.

"Thank you so much everyone," Natalie said. "Wyatt, for heaven's sake take a bow. This is Wyatt Cassidy, for anyone who didn't know. I have a feeling we'll all be waiting in line for his concert tickets one day."

Wyatt bowed and then gestured for her to come forward and bow, too.

Grinning at him, she did.

So many happy, encouraging faces smiled back. It made her feel like one of Nana's hugs.

Wyatt ran to sit with his family, while Sloane approached the makeshift stage.

"Everyone, this is Sloane Greenfield," Natalie said.

Sloane shook her head, but Natalie waved her up insistently.

"See how she doesn't want to come up here?" Natalie asked everyone. "But if it weren't for Sloane, all of this would have taken me years, or wouldn't have happened at all. Sloane was my real estate agent, but when she heard what I wanted to do she stepped down without hesitation and she's been working her butt off ever since to help make my dream a reality. And she wouldn't appear on Channel Twelve with me, or speak with the Trinity Falls Gazette, for fear of stealing one drop of the limelight from this project."

The crowd clapped for Sloane, even as she shook her

head and smiled at Natalie with her lips buttoned, like she wanted to scold her for this, but didn't have the heart.

"Well, Channel Twelve is here now," Natalie went on. "And I want everyone who sees this to know that when Sloane Grenfield says she loves this town, she means it. And her love is most definitely an action verb. Sloane, please let everyone know about tonight's donations."

She stepped back, forcing Sloane into the light, and truly hoped the woman got some business from this. Whether she wanted public credit for her work or not, she deserved all the recognition in the world.

"Okay, so everyone knows that we've applied for non-profit status, but we don't have it yet," Sloane said. "So, these donations may be tax deductible and they may not. Each and every one of you who made a contribution in your name can check with me anytime to find out the status."

"That's not why we gave," Shirley yelled out.

A few others yelled out their agreement and Sloane smiled out over the crowd, looking like she was finding her bearings.

"All of you came on strong tonight with your support of Carla's Place. And Natalie's grandmother would be proud - of the fact that her name was going on a piece of the town she loved, and of all of you for making it happen. The total of donations until about five minutes ago was truly incredible," she said. "In amounts small and large, you have gifted nearly two thousand dollars to this project. And that doesn't include the tickets or the silent auction, so we'll be updating you at the end of the evening."

There were cheers and whistles, but Natalie barely heard them she was so blown away by her neighbors' generosity. Tears blurred her eyes as she looked down into the crowd and saw Nana's friends smiling up at her.

"Then we received another gift, just after I totaled all of these," Sloane said. "The donor wishes to remain anonymous, and thanks to the rollicking good time that was being had on this stage, I believe they'll stay that way, because every eye was on Wyatt Cassidy."

There were a couple of approving whoops and another spontaneous burst of applause.

"That last gift was ten thousand dollars," Sloane said.

The room went silent.

"This amount was the entire budget for the first stage of the project," Sloane went on, a smile in her voice. "And it means that we can start work right away on Carla's Place."

35

SHANE

Shane watched Natalie on the stage from his place at the table between Wyatt and Rumor.

Rumor wiggled and smiled, and Wyatt nodded his head.

They were all happy for her.

Seeing her overcome with gratitude and excitement was contagious. The whole room felt like it was going to combust with the shared energy of everyone who was cheering for her.

"She did it," Wyatt said proudly.

"With your help," Shane pointed out. "Why didn't I know you could dance and sing like that?"

Wyatt shrugged, but he looked happy.

"It was really good of you to go up there and help her," Shane told him. "I'm proud of you, not just for your talent, but for using it when a friend was in need."

"You too, Dad," Wyatt said.

"What do you mean?" Shane asked him.

"I guess I was the only one in the room not looking at me when that last donation was turned in," Wyatt said.

Shane's heart pounded, but he would never lie to his son.

"Please don't tell her," he said after a moment. "I wouldn't want her to think... anything about it."

The speakers came to life with an upbeat Christmas song.

"If folks are in the mood, you can feel free to dance," Sloane announced.

Shane glanced up to see Natalie dragging Sloane onto the dance floor, the two of them laughing and chatting while they moved to the beat.

A few more people headed out, and soon the dance floor was hopping.

"You should ask her to dance, Dad," Wyatt said.

"She doesn't think of me that way, son," Shane said, feeling sad but resigned.

"You never actually watched that BeeBop video, did you?" Wyatt asked.

"Of course not," Shane said.

"I think you should," Wyatt told him. "Watch it from the beginning."

Shane waited as his son pulled out his phone, tapping and sliding until he found what he wanted. But Shane failed to see what the point of watching her be embarrassed like that could possibly be. He'd been there, and it wasn't easy to watch the first time.

"Here," Wyatt said, handing over the phone. "Rumor, want to dance?"

"Of course," Rumor yelled, as if she had been waiting for someone to ask.

The two slipped out to the dance floor hand in hand as Shane watched after them for a moment, smiling at the sweetness of it.

He turned his attention back to the phone, wondering again what in the world Wyatt thought he was going to see.

He tapped the *buzz* button, and the video came to life.

On the screen, the kid with the posters was asking the girl to the Snow Ball, just like he remembered.

But when he looked, just inside the frame, he could also see himself with Rumor and Natalie, talking at the table by the window.

He seemed to remember that he'd been telling her to hold out for decent wages, since there was so much work and so few workers this year.

But the audio didn't stretch far enough to pick up any of their conversation. Instead, he simply saw the two of them talking.

And he was suddenly breathless.

In the video, he was smiling down at Rumor while she unfolded the snowflakes.

But Natalie was looking at him.

Her expression was hard to describe in words, but in it he saw fondness, joy, and most of all, an undeniable longing.

She did care for him. She did want him. And that had been true since this video was taken. Which meant it had probably been true since long before then.

Had she felt this way back in school, when he so desperately tried to ignore his attraction to his best friend's sweet little sister?

Watching the look on her face, it all seemed so clear.

This was why his whole family knew she cared for him, too. This was the way she must look at him when he wasn't looking back.

And if he could just get out of his own way, maybe he

would get to see that expression in real life, instead of on a tiny screen.

Before he could change his mind, he got up, shoved the phone in his pocket, and stalked across the dance floor to find her.

The crowd seemed to instinctively sense his urgency, and a path opened up before him so that he could see Natalie, still dancing with Sloane Greenfield. Wyatt and Rumor had joined them, and they were all swaying, clapping, and smiling.

"Natalie," he said, realizing too late that his voice was too loud, too deep, that maybe he should have taken a breath first, or planned what he wanted to say.

"Shane," she breathed, looking up at him, the smile falling away from her face.

"Dance with me?" he asked, extending his hand.

Whoever had made the music playlist had chosen that moment to melt the upbeat holiday hit into a slow song.

She took his hand, and he pulled her close, losing himself in her hazel eyes.

"Thank you for being here," she murmured, after what to her might have felt like an awkward silence.

Shane could have gazed down at her beautiful face all night without a word spoken between them.

"It's an honor," he told her. "You've accomplished so much."

"This town has been very generous with me," she said, looking around at the crowd with an expression of wonder.

"You're working to do something that will benefit everyone," Shane said. "At the expense of your own inheritance."

He chose not to elaborate on how much she probably could have used the money from the sale of the house.

"And you made them feel good about helping," he went

on. "Look how happy everyone is. You made your dream into our shared dream."

She looked down and he knew she was embarrassed at his praise, but that she also drank it in because it was from him. Because she cared about him.

How could I have been so blind?

36

NATALIE

Natalie swept around the dance floor in Shane's arms, unable to believe it was really happening.

How many times in her life had she fantasized about a moment just like this one, with him gazing into her eyes like she was his world?

It was everything she had dreamed of.

And he was dancing her toward the sprig of mistletoe Betty Ann and her crew had hung as part of their work as the self-appointed decoration crew.

Natalie had laughed at them for doing it, and secretly worried how the three of them had managed it with nothing but a stepladder and a prayer.

But now that she and Shane were dancing toward it, she was glad it was there if it might be the spark that lit the fire between them.

Dr. and Mrs. Wilkinson danced underneath. The doctor pulled his wife close and dipped her before kissing her so passionately his glasses slipped down his nose. The crowd whistled and cheered.

Rumor and Wyatt were next, and Wyatt bent down so

that his little sister could kiss his cheek, to everyone's delight.

Natalie looked up at Shane, wondering if he would really kiss her. They were getting closer to the mistletoe, so close she almost couldn't breathe.

Five steps away, and his blue eyes blazed with passion as they met hers.

Four steps away, and her skin seemed to warm under his gaze.

Three steps away, and he allowed his right hand to slide up from her waist to tenderly cup her cheek, sending a shiver of rightness down her spine.

Two steps away, and she leaned into his touch, her heart pounding a frantic tattoo when his gaze lowered to rest on her mouth.

One step away and...

The lights suddenly came up, and the music went off.

"We have a special surprise for our organizer," Sloane said into the microphone. "Everyone, let's welcome our very special guest... Christopher Bell."

Shane dropped his hands from her, and she turned, unable to believe what she was hearing.

The crowd parted, revealing the incredible sight of her big brother, still wearing his fatigues, a smile on his handsome face.

"*Chris*," she yelled, barreling for him.

He wrapped his arms around her and lowered his face so she could kiss his cheek.

Just like Rumor and Wyatt, she couldn't help thinking to herself.

"This is quite a party, little sis," he murmured in her ear.

"I'm so glad you're here," she whispered back through happy tears. "How did you manage this?"

"I can't believe Cassidy kept it a secret," Chris laughed, pulling back to look at her.

"Wait," she said, "Shane knew you were coming home?"

"I asked him not to tell you," Chris said. "Because I wanted it to be a surprise. I'll be helping out on the farm, too."

"Oh, Chris," she cried, pulling him close all over again.

She could feel him laughing and shaking hands with someone who had come to greet him.

When she was able, she dried her eyes and turned around to see who it was.

Of course, it was Shane.

"You sure you don't want to stay at the house?" he was asking. "We've got extra beds."

"Nah, I like the Inn," Chris said. "But you'll see me every day, bright and early. Don't worry."

"City early or farm early?" Shane asked, winking at Natalie.

"What's that supposed to mean?" Chris asked.

"Cricket, is that your big brother?" Rumor demanded as she ran up.

"Did you know about this, too?" Natalie asked, shocked.

"I'm good at keeping a happy secret," Rumor told her with a serious expression. "But you can't keep other kinds of secrets from your grown-ups."

"Very true," Natalie told her. "Yes, this is my brother. His name is Chris."

"Pleased to meet you," Chris said, crouching to greet Rumor. "I heard you're good at making snowflakes."

"That's my big brother," Rumor said, pointing to Wyatt.

"The amazing cook, right?" Chris asked, standing and offering Wyatt his hand.

Wyatt flushed and shook it.

"Turns out, he's also a rockstar in the making," Natalie said. "But let's get you something to eat and drink, and we can tell you all about the party so far."

Chris wrapped an arm around her, and she led him to the table.

But it turned out that they didn't have much of a chance to chat, with what seemed like everyone at the party taking turns stopping by to fuss over him while he ate a hearty meal.

Natalie sat beside him, feeling proud and grateful to have her brother here with her.

Rumor was tucked into her other side, paging through a picture book with one hand and playing with Natalie's hair with the other.

Shane sat across from them, and Wyatt was leaning against the far wall, talking with a red-headed girl who looked like one of the Williams kids.

Though she mostly focused on her brother and their guests, once in a while, Natalie stole a glance across the table at Shane.

He seemed to never have his eyes off her for a moment.

"Thank you," she mouthed to him at one point.

He smiled back with such warmth in his blue eyes that she felt like her heart would overflow with happiness at having everyone she cared about right here in one room.

37

SHANE

As the evening went on, Shane's joy was at war with his guilt.

He was so proud of Natalie and all she had accomplished. And his heart was soaring at the look in her eyes moments before they were about to dance under the mistletoe.

But there was someone he had to speak with, someone to whom he owed the truth.

When her brother, Chris, got up to refresh his mug of apple cider, Shane followed.

"Hey, man," he said to his best friend.

But Chris never even broke his stride.

Shane could only assume Chris had guessed what was going on, and was hoping that if he kept his head in the sand he could wait it out, and the situation would go away.

But Shane had no intention of giving up so easily. He followed his friend doggedly, determined to do things the right way.

When they reached the table with the cider crock, Chris

ladled himself out a mug and then turned, his eyes flashing up to Shane's.

"You following me?" he asked.

There was an odd tinge of suspicion in his blue eyes, which looked more tired than they ever had before.

Shane was momentarily thrown.

"Let me guess," Chris said. "You wanted to talk to me about my little sister. After all, you gave her her a job."

Shane nodded slowly.

"And you gave her a place to stay," Chris went on.

"Yes," Shane said.

"And now, I'll bet you think she owes you something," Chris said. "And you've coming to me to tell me exactly what that is."

"It's not like that," Shane said, taken aback.

"Oh, it isn't?" Chris asked.

"Of course not," Shane said. "I would never. I respect her and care about her, more than you could know."

"I should punch you in the nose," Chris said.

Shane just gaped at him.

Though his reasoning was wrong, the long and the short of it was true. After hiring Natalie, working with her, and living with her, he had developed strong feelings or her. And while she owed him nothing, he longed to give her everything.

"I'm kidding, man," Chris said, barking out a laugh. "Besides, I've seen the way you two look at each other."

"Seriously?" Shane echoed.

"The way she's always looked at you," Chris said softly.

This wasn't the first time Shane had heard someone say this. But it was the first time he believed it.

A wave of awe and pleasure washed over him.

"I promise you that I will always treat her with kindness

and respect," he told Chris. "She will never want for anything."

"I'm not sure if you're looking for my actual blessing," Chris said. "Natalie is an adult, and it's up to her to choose what she wants. But if you're what she wants, I'm happy for you both, truly."

Shane stared at his best friend, unable to believe it could be this easy.

Chris pulled him in for a fierce hug.

"But if you ever hurt her," Chris whispered in his ear. "I will definitely kill you."

"Fair enough," Shane laughed, feeling his eyes burn with unshed tears. "Fair enough."

38

NATALIE

Back at Cassidy Farm a few days later, Natalie stood at the kitchen counter, with Rumor beside her on a step stool.

They were getting a special after-school snack ready for Wyatt. Natalie just hoped it would be enough to soften the blow.

She and Chris had spent the rest of the weekend at Nana's house, catching up and going through some of Chris's things. They had ordered pizza, listened to the music they'd loved during high school, and shared their favorite family memories.

It had been fun, healing, and heartbreaking, too. Chris had changed since going away, he was quieter now, and he had a tendency to think a moment before answering questions that she didn't remember from before.

Everyone changes, she reminded herself. *I'm probably different, too.*

But what hadn't changed was the bond that made being together feel like home. With Chris here, she felt whole again in a way she hadn't since losing Nana.

It wasn't until last night that she had started to really think about the situation with Shane again.

She had dropped Chris off at the Inn and headed to the farm, realizing she was going to see Shane this afternoon, and wondering what they might say to each other.

Her own feelings were overflowing her heart. After all, she had seen how he was looking at her, and felt his gentle touch as they danced.

But she also knew that time apart had likely reminded him that he wanted to stay true to the memory of his wife more than he wanted to start something new.

And if that was what he wanted, it would hurt, but she would keep holding back what was in her heart.

Everyone had been asleep last night when she slipped in and headed upstairs to bed.

The morning routine had gone just fine. Rumor wanted to talk endlessly about the fundraiser. They even planned to put their gowns on again for a tea party after pre-school.

But once Rumor was dropped off at school, extra groceries were bought, and dropped off at the Cassidy's and in Shane's own fridge because of the snow storm the newsman said was coming, Natalie was still stuck with an hour before it was pick-up time.

On a whim, she'd gotten out her phone and swiped for the BeeBop app to see if the fundraiser had gotten any attention. Ever since she had created the @WipeOutGirl profile to let people know about Carla's Place, she'd approached the app with excitement instead of dread.

Sure enough, she had a ton of notifications.

She clicked on the first one to see a text scroll that said *wipeout girl makes new friend omg wicked moves kid.*

The video behind it was her playing at the fundraiser with Wyatt singing his head off and dancing.

It had over a million views.

Another video was the same footage showing a split screen of Wyatt next to a black and white video of young Elvis Presley.

Hundreds of thousands more views.

She let the phone fall to the table.

How is this even happening? It seemed borderline impossible for a video involving her to be buzzing again. What were the chances?

But the chances didn't matter. It had happened, and this time Wyatt was on full display.

She buried her head in her arms and tried to think of what to do.

As far as she could tell, the videos were showing off Wyatt's skills, not making fun of him. But it was still a lot of attention for a very reserved young teen.

She knew how she had felt about her viral BeeBop, and she was an adult.

"Oh, Wyatt," she sighed. "You were only trying to help me."

She'd barely been able to pull herself together to pick up Rumor. And now that Wyatt's bus would arrive at any moment, she felt like her heart would beat out of her chest.

The front door opened and closed again and then footsteps clattered toward the kitchen.

"Wyatt," Rumor said happily.

The boy appeared in the kitchen, a happy smile on his face.

"Wyatt," Natalie said, coming out from behind the counter. "I need to talk to you about something. I want you to know I didn't plan it."

"I'm buzzing," he said with a big smile. "I know. It's so cool, right?"

"You're happy?" she asked.

"It's epic," he laughed. "The kids at school are calling me *Wyatt Riot* now."

Even though he was a teenager, and probably too big for cuddles, Natalie couldn't help flinging her arms around the boy for a quick hug.

He hugged her back, hard.

"Thanks, Natalie," he whispered to her. "You made me famous."

"We'll probably only be famous for a few days," she laughed, pulling back. "Unless you want to try to spin it into something more. I'm game to play for you anytime you want to sing, as long as it's okay with your dad."

"As long as what is okay with me?" Shane asked, his booming voice sounding happy as he strode down the hall to join them.

"Don't be mad, but I'm buzzing now too," Wyatt said.

"I really think they should change that verb," Shane said. "This means you're in a video, not that you raided Grandpa's liquor cabinet, right?"

"Yeah, Dad," Wyatt laughed. "There's a video of Natalie and me at the fundraiser going around. We were just talking about maybe making more videos, on purpose this time, if it's okay with you."

"That sounds like a fun project," Shane said. "But for now, I was hoping everyone could help me salt the walkways at our house and Grandma's. There's supposed to be quite a storm coming."

"Snow day!" Wyatt and Rumor yelled at once.

Shane smiled at Natalie over Wyatt's head, and she felt a wave of happiness flow through her.

The intimacy from the other night was still there. If anything, it shone warmer and brighter.

As they all bundled up, she was reminded of the feeling she used to have on Christmas Eve, when she and Chris were tucked in, but they could hear Nana bustling around in the living room.

Good and happy times were coming. She could taste them in the air.

39

SHANE

Shane looked around his living room in awe.

Snow fell steadily outside the windows, blanketing the farm in a mantle of shimmering white. The forecast said this was going to be a big one, but they were ready for it.

Inside, Natalie sat on the floor with Wyatt, helping him untangle strands of Christmas lights while Rumor laid out her favorite decorations on the coffee table. Now and then, she pointed out the very best ones, and Natalie stopped to admire them each and every time.

Christmas music played softly on the radio, and the air was rich with the scent of the gingerbread cake Wyatt had put in to bake before they started decorating the tree. Rumor was excited to help him with the frosting after dinner.

Shane felt like he was living in a fantasy of what the holiday should be. The only thing left undone was talking with Natalie.

Though no words or intentions had been spoken

between them, her eyes seemed to tell him all he needed to know. She cared for him, too.

He only hoped she liked him enough that she might be willing to have him - farm-hours, kids, and all. Though it had taken them what felt like forever to get to this night, he was dead serious about her, and he wasn't willing to compromise on that. They could walk down the path as slowly as she wanted, but he knew exactly where he wanted things to end.

The old-fashioned timer went off with a cheerful ding.

"My cake," Rumor said brightly, making Shane smile.

"I'll get it, guys," Natalie said, hopping up and jogging into the kitchen.

"Thanks," Wyatt said, then turned to his dad, his eyebrows raised in question.

Shane pretended not to notice.

"Did you ask her yet, Dad?" Wyatt whispered.

"Did you ask her on a date?" Rumor asked in a louder whisper.

Shane glanced through the arch into the kitchen, but Natalie was right next to the radio, and didn't seem to have heard.

"Not yet," he admitted to them softly.

"Why not?" Rumor asked, a sad expression on her little face.

"Well, I can't take her out on a date right now," Shane explained, pointing at the window. "We're snowed in."

"We could make a date night for you," Wyatt said thoughtfully. "Dinner's almost ready, and Rumor and I can fix dessert. The dining room can be the restaurant, and we'll serve you. And afterward, we can put a movie on for you right here."

Rumor started jumping up and down in place, her little hands covering her joyous smile.

"What do you think?" Wyatt asked.

"I think it sounds spectacular," Shane admitted, stealing another glance at the kitchen, where Natalie was placing the cake on a cooling rack.

It wasn't the most romantic plan in the world, but it was probably a pretty accurate look at what dating him would be like. And he could always take her for a fancy night out once the snow was cleaned up.

Though it wasn't rational to think that she would meet another man during a snowstorm, he was feeling eager to stake his claim, or at least declare his intentions.

"Do you think she would like an at-home date?" he asked the kids.

"*Yes*," Rumor squeaked.

"I really do, Dad," Wyatt told him. "She likes us too, and we're a package deal, right?"

Shane was taken aback at the hint of real worry he saw in his son's dark eyes.

"Wyatt," he said carefully. "This family will *always* be a package deal. And as far as Natalie? I'm honestly just worried that she likes you guys more than she likes me."

Wyatt's eyes crinkled with his smile and Shane pulled him in for a quick hug.

"Okay, guys, are we doing this?" he asked, turning to grab Rumor into the hug too.

"Natalie," Wyatt yelled over his shoulder. "My dad has a question he wants to ask you."

"What's up?" she asked with a smile as she walked back in.

Suddenly, the kids were scrambling to get away from

him, as if they instinctively felt that romance required privacy.

Though he noticed that they didn't go far.

He resisted the impulse to wink at them where they stood in the doorway, and turned his attention to Natalie instead.

Her dark hair was in a messy ponytail and there was a little flour on her sweater and jeans from helping Wyatt with the cake. She wore the same fluffy pink slippers on her feet that she'd had on the day he came to bring her home. She wore them around the house because they never failed to make Rumor laugh, especially when Natalie made them pretend to be piglets.

In Shane's eyes she could not have been more beautiful, even in her seafoam evening gown.

This was the girl he loved hanging out with in their school days, and the young woman he was getting to know all over again as he watched her love his kids. And the way she looked tonight was the physical embodiment of all that active love, a love so big it seemed to overflow from her and spill out onto anyone lucky enough to be in her life.

He wouldn't have her any other way.

"Natalie," he breathed.

She smiled at him and glanced over at the kids nervously.

"What's going on?" she asked.

The kids giggled.

"Shane?" she said.

"I know it's snowing out," he said. "But would you like to go on a date with me?"

For a moment her face went blank.

His blood ran cold.

She doesn't want me. She thinks I'm a terrible employer, trying to take advantage of her.

Then she broke into a great big sunny smile and her shoulders dropped.

"I would love that, Shane," she said, her cheeks turning pink. "When it stops snowing, I would love to go on a date with you."

"About that—" he began.

But Rumor burst into the room before he could continue, wrapping her arms around Natalie's legs and smiling up at her, her face lit up brighter than the tree.

"You can go on a date *here*," Rumor said. "We have movies."

"Oh, I like that idea," Natalie said. "After dinner, maybe we can set up the living room like a movie theater."

"I think your date should start now," Wyatt said. "Rumor and I will get the dining room all set up. Maybe you could meet each other there in ten minutes?"

"I'll pick you up in the hallway," Shane told her, hoping that was the more gentlemanly move.

"Thank you," she said, glancing at her slippers. "I'll just freshen up."

His heart threatened to beat out of his chest as he watched her climb the stairs.

40

NATALIE

Natalie sat at the dining room table half an hour later, laughing her head off as Shane told her a funny story about the time the horses got out and took a slow stroll across the Cassidy Farm parking lot just as the school buses were arriving for a field trip to the pumpkin patch.

Wyatt and Rumor were pretending not to watch from the kitchen counter as they ate their own dinner. She had invited them to join the date more than once, but they were very sure this was proper protocol.

Meanwhile, Shane was the ultimate gentleman. He had pulled out her chair for her and spent the meal asking her questions, and regaling her with funny stories, always making sure her wine glass was full of the lemonade Rumor had made from a mix she found in the cupboard.

"May we get these out of your way?" Wyatt asked politely when their plates were empty at last.

"Thank you," Natalie said.

Wyatt took her plate with a flourish.

Rumor took her father's plate, the silverware piled

precariously on top, and carried it very carefully to the kitchen.

"Dessert is served," Wyatt announced.

They each carried out a piece of gingerbread cake with a thick, if slightly uneven, cream cheese frosting, and placed them on the table.

"Oh, this looks lovely," Natalie told them.

"Wow," Shane said. "We're coming here more often."

She smiled at him, so glad he knew how to have fun with his kids.

"I mean, if you'd like to go on a second date, that is," he said, looking into her eyes.

She almost swooned under that piercing blue gaze, but managed to nod.

"Excellent," he said, his voice gravely and deeper than usual.

They ate their delicious dessert in companionable silence. Natalie managed to steal a glance at Wyatt and Rumor and give them two thumbs up for their baking and frosting skills.

When the meal was over, Shane pulled out her chair for her and gestured toward the living room, where the sofa awaited.

"One moment, please, miss," Wyatt said, then bent to whisper something to Rumor.

Rumor scrambled into the living room and fluffed up the throw pillows with great energy.

"Thank you," Natalie said. "This is a really fancy movie theater."

Rumor puffed up even more than the pillows at the compliment.

Natalie smiled as the kids flicked through the choices of

movies for her. Ultimately, she chose everyone's favorite animated fairytale, knowing they would be staying close.

"Not a scary movie?" Shane teased.

She grinned at him.

They sat down on the sofa, and the kids turned off the lights and scrambled onto the loveseat together.

As the movie began, she stole a glance up at Shane.

He smiled down at her and took her hand, wrapping it in the warmth of his.

A tingle of happiness went through her, and she squeezed his hand back, reveling in the gentle contact.

Everything was just right.

41

NATALIE

Natalie awoke on Christmas morning, wondering how it had come so quickly. She had been too busy enjoying a haze of happy, snowed-in days with Shane and the kids to really notice.

Each morning, while Shane battled the snow to tend to the horses and check on his parents, she and the kids worked on projects around the house - unpacking, hanging pictures, and of course the endless preparations for Christmas.

Two days ago, they'd unpacked the box she'd found before - the one with the picture of Shane and MaryLou. This time, Natalie felt like she understood that smile better. She hung it in the dining room, so MaryLou could still be a part of all those family dinners, and when she was finished, she stepped back to look at it, and made a promise.

"I'll take good care of them."

Shane noticed the picture while they were eating. He didn't say anything, but the way he smiled at Natalie told her all she needed to know.

During the last week, Rumor had learned to make paper

chains, and now the hall was hung with them. Wyatt helped her affix them in high places, and they both made piles of paper snowflakes.

They'd spent most of the afternoons, when Shane was back, baking piles of cookies and breads and listening to Christmas music, with the occasional "performance" by the kids when a particularly good song came on.

The Cassidys' new house really felt like a home now, Shane had said so last night during their movie.

Every night since their first date, they had watched a holiday movie, with the kids falling asleep on the loveseat beside them.

Natalie had grown accustomed to ending the night with Shane's big warm hand wrapped around hers. She could hardly expect a kiss at the end of their dates with so many little witnesses, but somehow, the feeling of their hands entwined was even better. It felt like a partnership, the two of them linked together to face the world.

She sat up in her bed and looked around the room. She hadn't been able to do much for the kids without the ability to leave the house for shopping. But she had written a special story for Rumor and a song on her guitar just for Wyatt. Those would have to do for now.

Just as she hopped out of bed, she heard little feet thundering up the stairs to her bedroom.

"Good morning, Rumor," she said, opening the door. "Merry Christmas."

The little one wrapped her arms around Natalie's waist and hugged her hard.

"Merry Christmas," she said, popping her head up so that her chestnut curls bounced around her shoulders.

"Is your brother up yet?" Natalie asked.

"Yes, he helped Dad with the horses," Rumor said.

"They're downstairs making French toast."

"Give me ten minutes to get ready, and I'll be down," Natalie promised. "I know you guys want to open your stockings."

An hour later, she sat at the dining room table, surrounded by sticky plates, open stockings, and happy faces.

Shane was smiling at her across the table like the cat that ate the canary. If he had a secret, she had no idea what it could be. She hoped he didn't have a gift for her, because she hadn't had time to do any shopping for him.

On either side of her, the kids were engrossed in their presents. Rumor was playing with her new toy trucks as Wyatt paged through a thick fantasy book.

Shane's phone rang, and he grabbed it.

"Hey, Mom," he said. "You ready for the rugrats to descend on you?"

He paused and then laughed.

"Merry Christmas to you, too," he said. "Okay, we're coming."

He hung up and turned to the family.

"Time for Grandma's?" Rumor asked hopefully.

"Time for Grandma's," Shane confirmed.

The kids exploded with excitement and dashed off to bundle up in their coats and boots while Shane and Natalie cleared the table.

"We do everything but the stockings at my parents' house," he told her. "I hope you don't mind."

"Not at all," she said. "But I feel bad. I couldn't really get out to get anything for you and the kids."

"Natalie," he said, putting down the towel he was holding to cup her cheek in his hand. "The only gift I want is time with you. And I know the kids feel the same."

A sizzle of electricity moved between them, and Natalie felt her cheeks heat.

"Are you ready to goooooo?" Rumor asked excitedly as she darted into the kitchen.

"Yes," he said, giving Natalie's cheek a tiny pat before letting go. "We just need to get bundled up, too."

They quickly pulled on boots and coats and headed out into the cold, crisp morning.

"The radio said the roads were finally being cleared between the village and the lake this morning," Shane said as they crunched through the snow. "Maybe your brother will make it over. I texted him already. My cousin Grace is staying at the Inn right now, too. I asked her to give him a ride if they both want to come, since she's got the Jeep."

"That would be amazing to see both of them," Natalie said, trying not to let herself get too excited. "I haven't seen Grace in years."

In spite of the cold, Mr. and Mrs. Cassidy were standing out on the porch, waving to them as they arrived.

"Grandma, Grandpa," Rumor yelled, dashing up the steps.

"Glad I salted those this morning," Shane murmured with a smile.

Her grandparents wrapped her in their arms and waited for Shane, Wyatt, and Natalie to join them before heading inside.

"It smells amazing," Natalie said.

"I made homemade doughnuts," Mrs. Cassidy told her. "But I was hoping you would help with the glaze. The kind you and Wyatt made for that lemon loaf the other day was so wonderful."

"I'd be glad to," Natalie said.

"I'll help," Shane offered, shooing Wyatt off.

That was a little odd, but Wyatt actually grinned at him and grabbed Rumor's hand to go choose a picture book to read with Grandpa.

Natalie and Shane had barely made it into the kitchen before her phone began to ring.

Expecting it was Chris, she picked up immediately.

"Natalie," Howie Linck said. "Merry Christmas."

"Oh, hello, Howie," she replied. "Merry Christmas to you, too."

She hadn't expected to hear from her electrician today.

"I just wanted to let you know I spoke with your general contractor, and we have a little Christmas surprise for you," Howie said. "The place isn't finished, but upstairs is ready for you to live in again. You can move back in tonight, if you want."

Shane gave her a questioning look.

"I can move back in?" she echoed.

Shane frowned.

"Yes," Howie said. "I thought you'd like to know. Merry Christmas."

"Merry Christmas," she replied.

She ended the call, and was hit with a feeling of sadness. Of course, it wasn't smart to be living with Shane while they were exploring their fledgling relationship.

But leaving him and the kids just felt wrong, even if she would be spending her days with them.

"Don't go," Shane said roughly.

"What?" she asked.

"Stay with us," he said. "Stay with me."

Out in the living room the kids were crowing with joy over their grandfather's jokes. The kitchen was warm and fragrant. And Shane's big presence in front of her brought her as much peace as longing.

"I know we're a lot," he said. "The kids are definitely a handful, and I'm always working. Maybe you would rather date someone who has more time to make you feel special. I would hate that, but I would understand. You deserve that, and more."

"You three make me feel special every single day," she told him, suddenly feeling fiercely protective of them all, and a little outraged that he would suggest his life made him less desirable. "There's nowhere I'd rather be."

"Then stay," he said again, a note of desperation in his voice she had never heard there before.

"It isn't right for me to live with you when we're dating," she said, repeating what she was trying to tell herself.

"So don't date me," Shane said, shrugging.

She blinked at him in confusion.

Then he was pulling something from his pocket and going down on one knee, and the whole world seemed to go blurry.

"Shane," she breathed, her vision clouded with happy tears.

"Natalie Bell," he said gently. "Will you marry me?"

The living room had gone silent. All she could hear was the drumming of her poor heart, which was ready to burst.

"Yes," she said. "Yes, yes, yes."

Shane slipped the ring on her finger, and she caught a sparkle of diamond and gold before he stood.

Then he was pulling her into his arms, one big hand cupping her cheek as if she were the most precious thing in the world.

Time seemed to stand still as he bent to bring his lips so close to hers.

His cerulean gaze moved from her lips to her eyes as if to ask permission.

She tilted up her chin and then his lips were crushing hers as he pulled her close.

Bubbles of happiness burst in her chest, and she kissed him back for all she was worth, feeling like the luckiest woman in the world.

Spontaneous applause reached her ears from the hallway, and she realized this was what Wyatt had been grinning about. Shane must have had this proposal planned all along.

She pulled back slightly, feeling shy about kissing in front of the kids.

Shane released her slowly, as if he was reluctant to stop kissing her. He kept an arm around her as they welcomed the family into the kitchen to congratulate them.

Rumor was the first to wrap her arms around them, then Wyatt.

"I'm so pleased for you both," Mrs. Cassidy murmured in Natalie's ear as she joined the group hug.

"Excellent news," Mr. Cassidy announced, clapping his son on the back and wrapping an arm around Natalie too. "It's good to have another happy face around here."

"Merry Christmas," a familiar voice called out from the living room. "We made it."

Chris.

"Sounds like your brother's here," Mrs. Cassidy said warmly, patting Natalie on the back. "And Gracie, too. Come on, everyone, let's go greet them."

As the others all trailed out of the kitchen, shouting greetings to the new arrivals, Shane pulled Natalie back into his arms and gazed into her eyes.

"I'm the luckiest man in the world," he told her. "I'll make sure you know how grateful I feel about that every single day."

"And I'm the luckiest woman," she replied with a smile.

He pulled her in for another kiss and she felt like the whole world had been spinning since the beginning of time just to place them in this moment, in this warm kitchen with the people they loved in the next room, in an ancient farmhouse, in a small town under a blanket of sparkling snow.

Together.

***

Thanks for reading **Cowboy's Christmas Nanny**!

Want to read Shane and Natalie's **SPECIAL BONUS EPILOGUE**? Sign up for my newsletter here (or just enter your email if you're already signed up!):
www.clarapines.com/cowboynannybonus.html

About the next book:

Are you ready to find out what's going on with Natalie's brother, Chris? Do you want to know the secret that got him sent home early, and learn what happens when a lost love from his past comes back to town with a VERY unexpected surprise?

If you want all that, plus an adorable baby, a lovable helper dog, and a cast of quirky characters all snowed in at the local inn as Christmas fast approaches...

Then check out **Soldier's Secret Baby** now:
https://www.clarapines.com/soldier.html

ABOUT THE AUTHOR

Clara Pines is a writer from Pennsylvania. She loves writing sweet romance, sipping peppermint tea with her handsome husband, and baking endless gingerbread cookies with her little helpers. A holiday lover through and through, Clara wishes it could be Christmas every day. You can almost always figure out where she has curled up to write by following the sound of the holiday music on her laptop!

Get all the latest info, and join Clara's mailing list at www.clarapines.com

Plus you'll get the chance for sneak peeks of upcoming titles and other cool stuff!

Keep in touch...
www.clarapines.com
authorclarapines@gmail.com
Tiktok.com/authorclarapines

facebook.com/ClaraPinesAuthor
twitter.com/clarapines
instagram.com/authorclarapines

Made in the USA
Monee, IL
26 January 2024